2022

The Return of the Annunaki

Robert Smith

Contact: atende@outlook.com

Facebook/RSAuthor

Visit: www.thekingsofayutthaya.com

Also, by Robert Smith

1809; The Year They Freed the Slaves
The Georgia Secession
The Pastor, The Atheist and the Unbeliever
The Will of the People

The Annunaki (Annunaki Book 1)
The Revenge of the Druids (Annunaki Book 2)
Deep State (Annunaki Book 3)
The Annunaki Novels (Annunaki Books 1 – 4)

South-East Asian Series

The Kings of Angkor
The Kings of Ayutthaya (published by Silkworm Books)
The Kings of the Toungoo Empire

The Tiger King of Siam

- *Chapter Ten* –

(From Book 1: The Annunaki)

The return of the Annunaki
2022

It started innocently enough. A comment was posted on the "Thinkers" Facebook page. "Is anyone sensing anything unusual?" it asked. Sales of this book went from two copies a week to over five thousand a day. Articles about the Annunaki started to appear in magazines and chatter increased on the Internet. Apart from the evidence of my bank balance, there seemed no rhyme or reason for the increased interest.

****

"It is time to return to planet Xra-343g in sector GF24S," thought the Commodore. Like his two fellow crew members who were not hibernating, he had reviewed the logs of the previous visit to the planet He need not, as the planet was one of the most interesting discovered and the subject of much speculation on Niburu. The memories of the first Commodore to visit Xra-343g were imprinted in his mind and those of his crew as he left the uninteresting Xpt-685b behind.

The spaceship slowed as soon as it picked up signals from Xra-343g.

"Hold a stationary position navigator Lon," thought the Commodore.

"The source of the radio waves is planet Xra-343g. There must still be life on the planet although not too advanced, or these signals would disappear as they entered their digital age," thought navigator Lia.

"They still existed when these radio transmissions were sent. The distance they have travelled makes the radio waves over one hundred years old. They are faint as is to be expected. The computer will enhance them and transfer them to us."

"Allow the computer to interrogate the transmissions. We will proceed slowly. These signals may allow us to build up a picture of life on this planet before our arrival. Wake the Dukaz and the Researchers. Their contribution and analysis will prove crucial," thought the Commodore.

"When the Dukaz and the Researchers are ready gather them in the briefing room," thought the Commodore.

The Annunaki gathered expectantly. The Commodore realized that it is often better to gather a group together. They can all interpret thoughts at a distance, but by gathering them together he reinforced their common objective.

"Planet Xra-343g is still circling its sun," he started. "It's atmosphere now shows higher levels of carbon dioxide, methane, nitrous oxide and ozone than was the case on our first visit. These changes may be due to natural phenomena on the planet's surface or may be due to the effects of industrialization, as was the case on early Niburu. As we get nearer the planet this should become clear.

We are receiving transmissions. Researcher Soa will lead the team evaluating the signals emanating from the planet, Researcher Mala will lead the team evaluating the condition of the planet, and Researcher Zal will lead the team examining how the life-forms we know as Hominin has developed and how they interact with each other.

I want to be fully briefed on all aspects before I make any decision on the possibility of revealing ourselves to them," thought the Commodore.

As the spaceship edged towards the Solar System Researcher Soa broke the news they had all been waiting for. The inhabitants of the planet had developed into a society capable of space exploration and had not only put spaceships into orbit but had landed on their moon. The grainy film of those first giant steps was enhanced and displayed throughout the Annunaki ship.

At the outer edge of the Solar System, they stopped. Information was flooding in to the ship's computers where they were analyzed and relayed. They stopped on the inner edge of the Kuiper belt with Pluto and Charon circling each other off to their right as they faced the sun.

"Commodore," thought Researcher Mala. "There is evidence that the humans (as they were now known on the spaceship) sent a probe to this dwarf planet recently."

"That is an impressive achievement for such a young civilization," thought the Commodore. "It shows that given their relatively young stage of development their technology has advanced at a pace beyond what we have seen on most other worlds." The Commodore turned to Captain Mir of the Ducaz.

"Capture that probe and bring it back here to be evaluated," he thought.

The Commodore then called the leaders of the three teams to the briefing room.

"I would like to gauge your early impressions on Xra-343g. I sense there is some concern over both the planet and the humans. It would be useful if I could gather your opinions," thought the Commodore.

"Our primary concern is that the planet itself is being over-exploited, as we evidenced earlier with our initial atmospheric analysis. They are releasing too much carbon back into the atmosphere causing a buildup of reflective gases in the upper atmosphere. The humans themselves, the plants and the trees are, like ourselves, carbon-based lifeforms. There was harmony in the carbon cycle until their period of industrialization. This has now been disrupted.

It is similar to early Niburu when our forefathers entered the industrial age. The difference is that we took action long before this point was reached. We made the birth of children against the law, set a maximum population for our planet and cleaned the atmosphere. They talk and achieve little. They scar the planet, the planet that supports them. There are nearly seven billion of the species on the planet. If we judge by the criteria that were applied on Niburu, we would set the planetary population limit at one billion to ensure sustainability," thought Researcher Mala.

"Researcher Soa, you have been working closely with Researcher Zal. What conclusions have you reached about the humans?"

"They are a highly complex species. As we witnessed on our first visit, they are capable of considerable self-sacrifice toward others. They evidence care towards their elders as they reach the end of their life-span and have developed medicines and treatments to care for the sick. In many ways they are a noble species," thought Researcher Soa.

"We implanted the thought DNA within the sample group. Is that not evident?" thought the Commodore.

"From what we can tell from here we can see little evidence of telepathy among those on the planet although we can sense some of them from here. It is possible some retain the power in a reduced form while for others it exists in the background. It may evidence itself in individuals from time to time. The DNA will be present in every human. It would have spread across the species many times as they evolved," thought Researcher Soa.

"There are historical stories that appear to show periodic attacks against those who evidenced thought. I, like others on the spaceship, have felt a connection with the planet which might evidence that the DNA still exists, but has been diluted over the millennia. We would need to examine a sample group to be sure," thought Researcher Zal.

"They trade between themselves using money. This, like many other aspects of their society, is an unknown to us and we are still trying to learn. A value is given and exchanges made. In one respect this money stabilizes their society, but in another it is causing fractures in the social fabric. It appears as if those who have large amounts of money are deemed more worthy than those who have little," thought Researcher Soa.

"We feel their society is fracturing and this has become more evident in recent years. The division of money is not equitable, and those who do not have sufficient are becoming more active against those who do. Unlike Niburu where the ruling council makes decisions, they are governed by over two hundred countries that are at different stages of development and have different amounts of money," thought Researcher Zal.

"One area that is causing much conflict is what they call religion. This is a concept we have struggled to grasp. It has been common throughout their development to worship "Gods" be they the Sun God, the Moon God or the one God. They appear to have myths and legends regarding ourselves and, at one time, worshiped us as Gods. We are still trying to evaluate this concept, but it could have severe implications for the planet if the divisions currently evident are not curtailed," thought Researcher Soa.

"The conflict over religion is a consistent theme throughout their history. Other conflicts arise over ownership of land and political ideology. These are all concepts with which we are unfamiliar and are trying to understand. The reason the conflict over religion concerns us is that they now have the power to destroy their planet. It appears as though previous wars have stimulated the growth in technology, weapons technology in particular. In our case, we did not discover nuclear power until the 23rd century in their terms. They discovered it in their 20th century," thought Researcher Zal.

"We had initial problems with what they call language. They communicate by speaking not by telepathy. This speech enables them to disguise their thoughts from others, and we have drawn the assumption that that this may lead to deception. It is clear from our initial observations that there is often a difference between what the humans say and what the humans do," thought Researcher Soa.

"They use language to communicate. There are thousands of different languages, and this has inevitably held back the development of the species. We have been examining one of the more common languages called English. It is very irregular and complex. It seems to have rules that contradict themselves, and it varies from country to country, but it does enable them to communicate freely using their speech mechanism," thought Researcher Zal.

"Captain Mir," thought the Commodore. "I require samples of their atmosphere for analysis. I also require twenty-five of these humans to be brought back to be evaluated by Researcher Soa and her team. Your presence is not to be detected."

"Yes Commodore," thought Captain Mir.

The group broke to continue their thoughts and to eat the delicious Alasay.

****

Billy-Bob Thornton was taking his one true love Penny for a drive in his lovingly restored 1962 Chevrolet Impala SS Convertible. It was early evening and the end of a hot summer's day as they drove down the back roads of Wichita, Kansas. In the twilight, Billy-Bob looked up to see what looked like a meteor shower through the clouds. Suddenly the car electrics failed, and the Impala slowly glided to a halt.

"Goddammit!" exclaimed Billy-Bob.

Out of the clouds emerged a silver disc. The disc hovered above them and emitted a red beam directly down on to the car. Billy-Bob, Penny, and the 1962 Chevrolet Impala SS Convertible were taken up into the body of the spaceship, screaming in terror.

Billy-Bob awoke in a silver room. He was restrained on the table but could see or feel no restraints. Three tall, thin, silver snake-like creatures entered the room in silence. Billy-Bob tried to move but was unable to move a muscle. They probed him with their implements for some time before taking samples of his bodily fluids. All types of his bodily fluids. He drifted into unconsciousness.

The following morning Billy-Bob and Penny awoke sitting in the Impala down the same back road.

"What happened," thought Penny.

"I'm not sure," thought Billy-Bob.

****

In earth terms, the Annunaki arrived at the edge of our solar system in 2016. The prophecies, of which there are many, said that they would return in 2022. The Annunaki had captured the public imagination. No one was sure why after all these years but in the three years since they settled near the Pluto - Charon system there had been an awakening in public consciousness.

Magazines appeared, the Internet continued to speculate, old books were released and new ones published. "The Return of the Annunaki" starring Tom Cruise and Jessica Barden was the biggest box office movie of all time.

****

The New Horizons probe was captured and returned to the Annunaki spaceship where it was taken apart and meticulously examined. To the Annunaki it was primitive but within it were ideas and concepts that the Annunaki had never considered. On board the probe they found a compact disc, a flag of the United States, a Florida quarter and the ashes of Clyde Tombaugh, the discoverer of Pluto. The Commodore, in particular, was moved by this gesture. That the astronomer who discovered the planet had had his ashes sent there. The commodore headed the team examining the probe and was beginning to realize that these were a species the like of which the Annunaki had ever encountered before.

Researcher Zal and her team examined the many cultures of the earth. They could see how the move from the rural economy to an industrialized one had fractured the family unit. To the Annunaki family was essential, and they struggled with the concept of people living alone. The Annunaki were never alone. Researcher Zal, in particular, became fascinated by the concept of humor, unknown on Niburu. She struggled to understand it, and she still struggles to this day.

The Commodore called his team together.

"Captain Mir, Researchers Soa, Zal and Mala thank you for joining me. I feel we are all conscious of the impact this particular mission is having on us. I sense an interest in this species that I have not felt before with any other," thought the commodore.

"It is more than an interest Commodore," thought Researcher Zal. "I feel, and I know others do that this particular species has awakened something in us."

"Yes, it is as though we have realized that our entire existence has been predictable. We live our lives together. The humans are individuals and act in unpredictable ways. They are capable of considerable kindness or unbelievable cruelty. We act for the good of all whereas they often act solely for the good of themselves," thought Researcher Soa.

"They have undertaken wars in the name of religion, greed, power or ideology. They have enslaved their own kind throughout their history. They place gold and jewels above people, and yet I remain intrigued by them," thought Captain Mir.

"I have given them much thought," thought the Commodore. "They are different from us in that they speak and we do not. By understanding each other's thoughts, our society works toward the common good of all. Perhaps in the past, those who thought differently were shunned, although that is only my supposition. Like Researcher Zal said I feel we have become predictable. Our fascination with the humans comes from the fact that they are unpredictable in so many ways and yes, I can sense it as can you; we would like to emulate some of their ways."

"We know these thoughts will be read by others of our kind. We will have to see how our people react when we return," he added.

"And what of the humans Commodore?" thought Researcher Mala.

"We must do all in our power to see that they do not destroy themselves," thought the Commodore. "I feel it is best that do not reveal ourselves to them. They need to mature as a species before we can interact with them in any meaningful way."

"I would like to stay," thought Researcher Soa. "We have been in orbit for three of their years. We are part of their DNA. It is as if that link remains in their memory. If you monitor what they call entertainment there are movies about us, books being issued, and we are the subject of much debate. This recognition of us is unparalleled since the early days of their civilization."

"I too would like to stay," thought Captain Mir. "I have reconnoitered the Solar System. I would suggest that we establish a base on either the fourth planet, the one they call Mars. Its gravity is 0.77 Niburu, and has no appreciable atmosphere but it is stable. We can remain there undetected until their explorations reach the planet."

"I too would like to stay," thought the Commodore. "But that is not possible. I must return to Niburu with the spaceship. It is unprecedented to leave a colony behind, but the circumstances are exceptional. This species must be allowed to develop, and we are the guardians of their survival."

"Captain Mir, you are to ensure that no asteroid, comet or other body impacts the planet. Captain Mir select five of the Ducaz. Researcher Soa I will leave with you a contingent of twenty Researchers. There will be many volunteers.

"I fear for the humans. I ask you to take, what you consider to be the best course of action to stop them from destroying themselves. You understand that it will be another million years, at the earliest, until we return. If the Ruling Council does not agree with what we report we may never return," thought the Commodore.

"The Ruling Council will agree," thought Researcher Soa. "And I, and my descendants, expect to be visited by a far different Annunaki than we are today upon their return."

Chapter 1

Joel woke up with a start. He was dripping with sweat despite the cold Chicago winter.

"Again," said Michael his longtime lover.

"It's the same dream but it's not the same dream. I'm not even sure it's a dream it just feels so real. I'm there amongst them as they think. It's like I am on a spaceship or in something enclosed, but surrounded by thoughts. I can't see them, I can only hear them," Joel said.

"Maybe you should go and see a doctor. This is happening every night now, said Michael.

"And tell him what? That I am dreaming of aliens every night," replied Joel as he lay back down on the bed. "It's what they are talking about. I hear them all so clearly."

"And what are they talking about?" asked Michael.

"They are talking about us, the human race. They see us as some sort of experiment that has gone wrong. It's as if they are evaluating our future. Whether we should live or die," said Joel as he looked into the blackness. "I just can't get my head around it," he said as drifted back to sleep.

"Tell me more about the voices?" asked Michael as he placed two freshly squeezed glasses of orange on the breakfast table.

Joel looked up. It was obvious to Michael where his brain was.

"Oh, it's difficult and I don't get it. It's like there are a hundred people talking all at once but they make no sound. What's worse is that I am not only hearing this in dreams. If I go somewhere quiet, I can hear them talking, well thinking, during the day. The conversations go on relentlessly. It has only started following President Obama's revelation confirming the existence of aliens," he said. "I must be going mad, mustn't I? Last night they were talking about a Burman king, King Bayinnaung whose armies swept through South-East Asia in the 16th century. I've never even heard of him. I checked him out on the Internet when I woke up and there he is. How the hell do I know this?"

"I tell you what, we can go and see that new Tom Cruise 'The Annunaki' movie after work. That'll help take your mind off things. It's getting really good reviews."

They left the movie theater and went into a downtown bar. The bar was a bit country but neither of them minded that.

"It's nothing like the Annunaki," said Joel.

Michael was tempted to say 'what are you talking about' bur realized it would be better to allow his boyfriend to continue.

"The Annunaki are not warlike, they have no desire to conquer and enslave us. Quite the reverse in fact, they made us into what we are and they want us to succeed but they are very worried about us and what we are doing to the planet," said Joel.

Joel looked up at Michael conscious of what he had just said.

"Tomorrow we go and see Maximilian Browne," said Michael.

****

The Commodore was ready to depart on his return journey to Niburu, a voyage that would take half a million years.

"I am concerned that what we have learned from the humans will impact the behaviour of the crew, particularly on so lengthy a trip," he thought.

"I share your concerns," thought Captain Mir. "The mental stability of the crew is a new factor, one we as a race have never faced before. It is as if exposure to the culture of these humans has infected them."

"The entire crews' thought processes have been stimulated in a new series of directions. It is difficult to predict the outcome. You can hear their thoughts, they are not always the inquiring and analytical thoughts of the Annunaki, now they are interspersed with random thoughts ranging from wars to jazz. It is not the way of the Annunaki," thought the Commodore.

"The Annunaki know a closeness, a bond, that these humans do not have. Speaking allows you to mask your true intentions as we can see from our studies of their planet. Thoughts are transparent, they are not opaque. They are what they are," thought Captain Mir.

"The crew know of my concerns as do you. They can hear what I am thinking as I can hear their thoughts, my concerns echo theirs and their most important concern is that they may never see home again, never see their families again, as I may decide to destroy our spaceship rather than risk infecting Niburu with the worst aspects of the humans," thought the Commodore.

"You have a journey of half a million years ahead of you. Time enough to decide," thought Captain Mir.

"But decide I must," thought the commodore. "You have completed your preparations?"

"I have selected from among the Ducaz and Researcher Soa has selected her team. Navigator Lon has asked to stay and I have told him he is welcome. I feel his skill in piloting the sub craft will prove invaluable as the situation on the planet is one of concern," thought Captain Mir.

"Their planet is at a tipping point, and although some can see it, others deny or obfuscate either for their own self-interest or from some sense of ideology," thought the Commodore. "You have two areas to evaluate, the first is the environment of the planet and how it can be brought back from the edge, and secondly, their society itself that appears to be fracturing and tearing itself apart. You need to understand both the planet and the people."

"They have an understanding of how they are impacting the environment of their planet and there are many advocates who are putting forward solutions but not all listen or want to listen. They have faced global threats before most notably when two nations faced each other with the threat of nuclear war but held back on the brink of certain destruction. What they face now is different with societies dominated by religion and others by an increasing need to look inwards," thought Captain Mir. "It is difficult for us to comprehend."

"But comprehend you must. I leave the well-being of this planet and the humans in your hand. The decisions you make will be those of you and your crew alone. I guide you in one way, the humans have much merit but also an ability to destroy, you must find a balance. The planet can be saved and the environment repaired if they were absent. The planet, a planet of such beauty that it takes my breath away to this day, must be saved," thought the Commodore.

"It may be that our original explorers all those millions of years before selected the wrong species. The record show that they had to decide between the early hominids that developed into the humans of today or a species of insect known to the humans as a praying mantis. We will look again at this species to see if, over time, it could become a suitable replacement. As you say it is the planet that must be saved," thought Captain Mir.

They were interrupted by a voice outside their conversation.

"We are ready to depart," thought navigator Gon. "Their probe has been released to continue its journey."

"My sub craft and its outriders are ready to travel inwards to the fourth planet where we can establish our base. We will continue to monitor the planet and try to understand the humans, their religions, their cultures and their politics. We need to fully understand them before we interfere in any way," thought Captain Mir.

"You have one small advantage that we did not have until recently, that, the existence of aliens has now been acknowledged," thought the Commodore.

"I wish you and the Annunaki well on your return journey Commodore," thought Captain Mir.

"And I you," thought the Commodore and that thought was echoed throughout the spaceship between those staying and those going.

****

The auditorium hushed as Maximilian Browne, tall, thin and with his long, black beard hanging down the front of his white kaftan entered onto the stage and took his position behind the lectern.

"Fellow thinkers," he began. "Finally, the government have admitted to their gross cover-up of what we all knew to be true all along."

"The words brought alive to us in the writings of Zechariah Sitchin in his *Earth Chronicles* have now been proven to be true. That the Annunaki altered our DNA to create mankind in order that man could serve them is now a scientific fact. The famed Researcher Matthew Wright, a man who gave his life to ensure the government no longer kept the facts from us, has shown us the inequity of our government. We have been ridiculed and suppressed over many years but now the truth is out there for all to see!"

The audience rose to their feet and clapped loudly. This was the firebrand Maximilian Browne they had come to see. The leader of the Annunaki religion, now able to operate freely in the world.

"Yes, brothers and sisters, from the time of the Mesopotamian's and going far back beyond that the Annunaki have watched over us. The legend tells of them enslaving early man to mine for gold and other precious minerals. We have no way of knowing. What we do know is how those early religions worshipped them, even before God!"

"The Annunaki, 'the seed of Anu', and 'those of princely blood' are 'the Sumerian deities of the old primordial time'," as Zechariah Sitchin told us all those years ago, only to be held up and ridiculed by the world at large, but we, brothers and sisters, we he held the faith despite the naysayers only to be proven right. The Annunaki, the children of the sky god Anu and Ki, the Sumerian mother goddess Ninhursag and the Babylonian and Akkadian goddess Antu and the consort of the god Anu. A union between a god from the skies and a mortal female. How blessed were their offspring?"

"Ki, the name, the symbol, that Sitchin proves is the Sumerian for Earth, our planet, the planet that nourishes and feeds us, the planet that allows us to breed and worship the Annunaki in the ever-increasing numbers that I see before me today. Their offspring born of a God and a mortal woman walk the Earth. Their blood is in all of us, their DNA is in all of us."

"The Nephilim, one of the first records from the Book of Enoch, a book for centuries decried by the established religions as an apocryphal text, represents nothing more than suppression of the truth, similar to the suppression of the truth that our government has put before in recent years," he added in a quiet voice. "Our government has admitted the truth and now is the time for those established religions to do the same!" he said raising both arms in the air and challenging the accepted religions.

As the crowd rose, he hushed them and continued.

"The early church accepted the book of the patriarch Enoch. Fathers of the Christian faith, Clement of Alexandria, Tertullian, and Irenaeus amongst them accepted the book of Enoch. Copies of the book were found in the Dead Sea Scrolls and Enoch is quoted in the Book of Jude and referenced throughout the Bible. The Book of Enoch tells of an event, an event before the Deluge when two hundred fallen angels, the Watchers, led by the angel Semyaza, gathered on Mount Hermon and swore to father children with human women. The Hebrew texts refer to these children as 'the Nephilim'. Who is to say that this is not evidence of the return of the Annunaki? Who is to say they visited us only once? Enoch records that they fathered a race of great giants who 'consumed all the acquisitions of men' before humans turned against them. Who is to say this was the Annunaki? Who is to say whether this was another race of aliens who have visited us in the dim and distant past? The address by the president acknowledged no fewer than five different alien species have visited us. Who after all this time can know the truth?

The silence in the auditorium verged on rapture as he continued.

"The Epic of Gilgamesh, according to the widely respected scholar Edward Lipinski, places the cedar forests of Mount Hermon and Lebanon as the dwelling place of the Annunaki. No longer can this scholarly work and so many others be dismissed. The government has acknowledged the existence of aliens. Now we can evaluate such research in a new light.

"I quote to you from Edward Lipinski's work," said Maximilian Browne as he put on his heavy black glasses to read. *"traces of the older tradition can be found in the mention of the mountain which was the abode of the gods, and whose accesses were hidden by the cedar forest whose guardian was Humbaba. This mountain was we believe, the Anti-Lebanon-Hermon ... The southern range of the Anti-Lebanon is therefore likely to be the mountain in whose recesses the Annunaki dwelled according to the Old Babylonian version of the Gilgamesh,"* he quoted. "I ask you to remember that in this period the Annunaki were regarded as gods. Mount Hermon was the dwelling place of the gods. It is only time and the stories of man that have taken us in a different direction and to a different God. The prophesies tell of their return in the year 2022 and we will be waiting to welcome them home!"

The audience rose as one. This is why they were here. To hear the word from the voice of their new religion.

****

Joel's face was ashen as they left the theatre. "They don't understand. They don't understand any of it," he said.

They walked side by side, in silence, until they turned into Zanzibar, an African themed bar and restaurant.

"What can I get you gentlemen," said the waitress.

"Two deluxe big Z burgers both medium with diet Cokes," said Michael.

"What don't they understand?" he asked.

"I know I'm not mad. I don't know why but I understand things, things I can't possibly know or understand. I know about the Annunaki, they talk to me and now I know why," said Joel. "they are telepaths and they engineered some humans to be as they are."

"Then why aren't I able to hear them?" asked Michael.

"Because over millions of years those who were telepaths bred with those who weren't and the ability was diminished over time. I kid you not, telepaths were persecuted in the past and had to hide their ability but some remain, and I am one," said Joel. "I know this sounds utterly ridiculous but after tonight I understand. I can't thank you enough for taking me."

"Two cokes and your burgers will be right along," said the waitress.

"I know I'm not mad because I sensed another telepath in the auditorium who is discovering her new found abilities just as I am. I am in contact with her now and, I daresay, we will be in contact forever. It seems to be the way it works. The Annunaki mother ship has returned to Niburu but those who remained will still be in contact with those returning for a distance of up to ten light years."

"You are right, it does sound utterly ridiculous and if I didn't know you better, I would dismiss what you said as the ravings of a madman but I believe you, although I would caution you not to speak of this outside us two," said Michael.

"Two Big Z's," said the waitress.

"What did you mean when you said that they don't understand?" Michael asked.

"I was listening to Maximilian Browne, an excellent speaker but a complete charlatan. He was telling of the history as recorded in the annals, of the Epic of Gilgamesh and of the book of Enoch. I don't dispute that he knows the legends and has mastered them for his audience, but now even he has doubt. I could sense it."

"But he is world famous as the voice of the Annunaki," said Michael.

"As the Annunaki get nearer their presence becomes stronger and their message becomes better understood," said Joel.

"Top up those cokes for you?" asked the waitress not waiting for a reply.

"Getting nearer?" asked Michael.

"They are on Mars now, watching us, learning who we are," said Joel.

"The other telepath you mentioned they can't be the only one sensing that the Annunaki are getting closer. There must be more of you," said Michael.

"I think you are right but I can only sense one person so far. I need to be careful in revealing what I know," said Joel.

"And what is it you know?" asked Michael.

"You are to tell no one. That the Annunaki are looking at our species to evaluate whether we should still exist on Earth, or will our disregard for the environment and ever-expanding population be unsustainable over time. Their interest is in us, but their over-riding concern is the well-being of the planet. We can be replaced, the planet cannot.

Chapter 2

"My God!" exclaimed Clyde Whittaker as he took his feet off his desk where he had been idly watching the computer screen. "It's the New Horizons probe. It's back!"

"What are you talking about?" asked Jenny Claybourne from the other side of the empty operations room. "We lost contact over three months ago."

"Look on the screen. It's there, and it's signalling back," said Clyde.

"That's the probe's signature alright. How can it be?" asked Jenny as she rushed across to Clyde's workstation.

"I don't know. It vanishes for three months and then reappears on our screens. It makes no sense," said Clyde.

"Look at the time the signal took to arrive at earth. It is the same time as when we lost the signal," said Jenny.

"But that can't be, can it?" asked Clyde.

"No, it should be much further out. How can it be in the same place?" asked Jenny.

"We need to double check this. There is no way that it could have stopped for three months and then resumed its speed and trajectory, let alone stared sending messages back again," said Clyde.

"Boss, New Horizons is back," Clyde shouted as William Manners entered the office carrying his sixth coffee of the day.

"What?" he asked.

"New Horizons is back, you are going to want to see this," said Clyde.

William, Clyde and Jenny stared at the computer screen not believing what they were seeing. Fifteen minutes later another signal came in.

"You guys are right. How on Earth can this happen. It's at the same position that we lost it three months ago. This will take some thinking about. I've no idea how we will present this to the press," said Boss William Manners.

The press gathered in the news room as they had many times before. The journalists filed into the small auditorium where NASA held most of its briefings. Many of them had been covering the activities of the space program for many years and were a little surprised to receive a call for an urgent update from the New Horizons team.

"Do you have any idea what this is about?" asked Marcia Pearce of the Orlando Guardian.

"None at all. I received the invite yesterday and here I am. They wouldn't give any details which makes the meeting a bit of a mystery," said Peter Duckworth of the L.A. Chronicle.

"It is a mystery," said Marcia. "The New Horizons probe suddenly stopped transmitting three months ago just after it passed Pluto. They put it down to a malfunction and the program was stood down. Why now?

Four NASA scientists entered onto the stage and took their respective seats. With the NASA logo behind them and their nameplates in front of them they sipped their water and prepared to announce their findings to the world.

"That's Johnathon Langerhans, the Administrator," said Marcia to Peter Duckworth who was sitting next to her.

"Well, this must be more important than we thought," replied Peter. "To get briefed by the head of NASA must mean this is something pretty important."

"Good afternoon, Ladies, Gentlemen and members of the press and thank you for attending at such short notice," said Johnathon Langerhans. "For those of you who don't know me I am Johnathon Langerhans the Administrator of NASA and alongside me are the three remaining members of the scaled-down New Horizons team, Director William Manners, flight controller Clyde Whittaker and Dr. Jennifer Claybourne." They each indicated themselves with a slight raise of their hands as their name was mentioned before the Administrator continued. "I hand you over to the Director of the New Horizons program, William Manners."

"Thank you, Administrator," said Bill Manners. "Like the rest of the world we thought that the New Horizons program was finished. Transmissions from the probe halted abruptly slightly over three months ago and apart from my small team of three who were collating and finalizing all the data, we were drawing the operation to a close. It was assumed that the probe had suffered a malfunction and despite our best efforts all contact with it was lost. That was until last Tuesday when our flight controller Clyde Whittaker saw a blip on his computer screen. New Horizons is back. I hand you over to Clyde."

"The reason you are here today is, yes to receive the good news that New Horizons is back and working perfectly, but also to be made aware of an anomaly that has occurred which at the moment we are at a loss to explain. We lost New Horizons shortly as it left the Pluto-Charon system. On Tuesday we received our first signal back from the tiny spacecraft. I was in the office with Jenny, Dr. Jennifer Claybourne, and as we watched the signals arrive and checked the telemetry, we were quickly aware of an anomaly. The signal was taking approximately the same time to reach Earth as it did when the spacecraft ceased transmission," said Clyde looking to Jenny on his left.

"This made no sense to us and Clyde and myself waited for more data from the spacecraft which enabled us to confirm our findings. At that point we called Director Manners to discuss what we had found. All three of us were at a loss to explain how after three months the New Horizons probe had reappeared at the spot where communications had ceased. As we continued to monitor the spacecraft it became apparent that it was traveling at the same speed and on the same course and trajectory than before communications had been lost," said Jenny.

The auditorium was silent as the press corps digested the news. Marcia raised her hand and Bill Manners indicated for her to ask a question.

"Can I clarify what you are saying? The spacecraft is back in perfect working order but is still at the same spot it was three months ago," she asked.

"And it is traveling at the same speed, course and trajectory as it was," said Director William Manners.

"But that makes no sense," said Marcia. "Where has the spacecraft been for the last three months?"

"That is why we made the announcement today. At present we have no logical answer, but it is fact the New Horizons probe is back and working normally," said Director William Manners.

"Newton's first law of motion states that an object will not change its motion unless a force acts on it," said Peter Duckworth. "How can you explain the appearance of the probe traveling at the same speed and trajectory?"

"At the moment we can't," said Director Manners.

"Aliens," joked Byron Marshall of FOX News.

****

The sub craft uncoupled from the underside of the mother ship. At five football pitches in length and seven layers in height the sub craft was the archetypal UFO of human imagination. A crew of four hundred volunteered to stay behind in order to try and save the humans from themselves despite the fact that they knew that they would never see their home planet again. Captain Mir guided the sub craft towards Mars inward passing by Saturn and Jupiter in the distance.

"Navigator Lim, we need to find a suitable landing spot way from the line of sight of the probes of the earth satellites monitoring this planet," thought Captain Mir.

"Their satellites photograph the planet on various frequencies to ascertain the make-up and increase their understanding. What they are doing is similar to our first ventures into space on the planet Coroya. To remain undetected is simple as their probes are not particularly sophisticated and we can easily avoid them," thought navigator Lim.

"We will draw auxiliary power from their sun while on the surface. There is more than enough sunlight reaching this planet that we can exist without using our power reserves. Put us down on an open plain to maximize our exposure to the sun. we are likely to be here for many years," thought the captain.

As the sub craft landed it came into its own. The spaceship was designed as a support vessel for the mother-ship and was fitted out with all the necessary facilities to carry out detailed research and analysis both at a distance and on planet Earth, if it proved necessary. Navigator Lim landed her without disturbing a grain of Martian dust.

The Annunaki had studied the Earth from their vantage point near Pluto for nearly three years and as they landed on Mars their proximity to Earth meant that more of those people susceptible to their aura could feel their presence.

"Researcher Soa, we will waste no time. The Ducaz are keen to involve themselves in this project. They will journey to Earth within the hour and bring back live samples for you to examine," thought Captain Mir.

"Excellent, we will ready the laboratory. It is important that complete sterility is maintained and that they do not come into contact with either us, or the Martian atmosphere," thought Researcher Soa.

"Any cross-contamination will mean that the samples will have to be destroyed," thought Researcher Zal.

****

Billy-Bob Thornton was taking his one true love Penny for a drive in his lovingly restored 1962 Chevrolet Impala SS Convertible. It was early evening and the end of a hot summer's day as they drove down the back roads of Wichita, Kansas. In the twilight, Billy-Bob looked up to see what looked like a meteor shower through the clouds. Suddenly the car electrics failed, and the Impala slowly glided to a halt.

"Goddammit!" exclaimed Billy-Bob.

Out of the clouds emerged a silver disc. The disc hovered above them and emitted a red beam directly down on to the car. Billy-Bob, Penny, and the 1962 Chevrolet Impala SS Convertible were taken up into the body of the spaceship, screaming in terror.

Billy-Bob awoke in a silver room. He was restrained on the table but could see or feel no restraints. Three tall, thin, silver snake-like creatures entered the room in silence. Billy-Bob tried to move but was unable to move a muscle. They probed him with their implements for some time before taking samples of his bodily fluids. All types of his bodily fluids. He drifted into unconsciousness.

The following morning Billy-Bob and Penny awoke sitting in the Impala down the same back road.

"What happened," thought Penny.

"I'm not sure," thought Billy-Bob.

****

"How are the examinations progressing?" thought Captain Mir.

"The Ducaz have brought back twenty of the required twenty-five samples to date. The humans have been selected from random areas throughout the populated areas of the planet and, although it is only a small sample, it will enable us to carry out a full DNA and intelligence analysis while enabling medical research," thought Researcher Soa.

"Will they be able to remember anything when they return?" thought Captain Mir.

"The answer to that should be no," thought Researcher Soa. "But there are earth records that show the previous humans taken from the planet have remembered fragments of their experience. We are not sure how or why this happens," thought Researcher Zal, interrupting the thoughts of Researcher Soa.

"Researcher Zal is right. Their minds are wiped clean by the final scan but it seems as though, with this particular species, the examination sometimes leaves an imprint in some of their memories and has consistently done so over the millennia of our visits. Their films and books on the subject of aliens often depict spacecraft similar to ours along with long, thin, grey aliens that, I imagine, are meant to depict us, or another species that may have visited the planet," thought Researcher Soa.

"I was surprising that the President of the United States admitted to the existence of aliens after many years of denial and he said that there was evidence in the form of spaceships that at least five different alien species had visited the planet. "We have encountered only two other inter-galactic civilizations on our journeys. It would be interesting to examine the craft of the other civilizations," thought Captain Mir.

"We have been studying the planet for some time now and there is no doubt we have found the humans interesting, but also on the cusp of destroying their planet. We must not allow to happen," added Captain Mir.

"I am sensing that there are still some on the planet capable of telepathy," thought Researcher Soa.

"I sense that very weakly as well. It might be that now we have moved in to the fourth planet that our proximity to Earth may make those who have the ability sense us more clearly," thought Captain Mir.

"There can be little doubt that our proximity at the edge of their Solar System awakened something in them, you can see it in their social connectivity. The humans carry the DNA we implanted all those eons ago, and that DNA would not have degraded over time but would have passed through their population. It may have been diluted after inter-breeding between those with our DNA and other humanoids or humans over time, but the DNA remains," said Researcher Soa.

"What is important for us is that these who retain their telepathic ability are identified. To have a telepathic link to someone on the planet could prove of considerable importance as we seek to know more about the humans and what motivates them," thought Captain Mir.

"Yes, to understand their thinking without them hiding behind the veil of talking will give us a much better insight into our understanding of them," thought Researcher Soa. "We are seeing only three humans exhibiting clear telepathic powers and all three started to sense us when we were in our old orbit around the Pluto-Charon system, but now we are closer I would anticipate more of those with remaining telepathic abilities to become aware, though to what extent it is hard to say."

"In addition to your responsibilities with regard to the specimens being brought back I would like you to set up a team to monitor those we know to be telepaths and those who are beginning to exhibit telepathic power, Oh, I see you already have," thought Captain Mir.

"I have already given the role to Researcher Zal," thought Researcher Soa.

"Already one of the telepaths, a human male named Joel, has made strong contact and is already aware of where we are and what our mission is. A female, named Belinda, is also beginning to make good contact although Joel is by far the stronger of the two.

They both attended a presentation on The Annunaki, as they perceive us to be in their history, given by Maximilian Browne yesterday in Chicago in the United States of America. The presentation showed how the myths and legends about us have been integrated into their creation mythology and beyond. The girl, Belinda, travelled from her home in New York to attend. Joel lives in Chicago. I know that Joel sensed Belinda's presence but I couldn't ascertain if they had made direct telepathic contact, I think not at this stage," thought Researcher Zal.

"And the third telepath," thought Captain Mir.

"Is probably the most interesting. Alessandra D'Angelo is an Italian environmentalist who is well-known internationally. She currently exhibits a certain amount of reluctance to acknowledge his telepathic powers and, as both Joel and Belinda did in the early stages, she thinks she may be going mad. It seemingly takes time for the humans to adjust when their latent abilities are awakened," thought Researcher Zal.

"But they do adjust, or so it would appear," thought Researcher Soa.

"Why do you find this Alessandra D'Angelo is the most interesting?"

"In their hierarchy they have many sub-cultures that it is difficult for us to understand. One that both Researcher Soa and myself have struggled with is what they refer to as 'the cult of celebrity.' The mass of the people follows sports stars, musicians, or actors or actresses often to the point of idolizing them. In some ways you can compare it to those we hold in high esteem on our home planet, but often with greater intensity," thought Researcher Zal.

"But these people add nothing of substance to the development of civilization. We hold those who excel in the sciences, in engineering, in the development and advancement of our race in high esteem, not those who excel at trivial pursuits," thought Captain Mir.

"It could be said that these people enhance their culture and allow them to establish a national identity, or a common bond. It appears trivial to us but has considerable significance to the humans," thought Researcher Zal. "Because there are so many of them infesting the planet their society is broken down into numerous units called countries, each with its own distinct identity. They coalesce around this identity in many cases. To get back to your question about James Yang. I consider him the most important of the three as he is one of those people, rare in their society, he is a proven scientist yet is also regarded as a celebrity in his part of the world. His word carries weight," said Researcher Zal.

"Only three among a population of nearly seven billion can be identified as telepaths so far, perhaps now we are closer to their planet more will rediscover their gift," thought Captain Mir.

"We know our ancestors enabled those they chose to have the power of telepathy but time has done the reverse of what our pioneers hoped. They wished for a telepathic species but subsequent visitations recorded a high level of persecutions against telepaths over the many millennia," thought Researcher Zal.

"All the species we have encountered on our travels across the galaxy are telepaths. I have studied the sample groups returned so far and I have examined past records, and one fundamental problem stands out, the ability to talk gives you the power to deceive. They say one thing and mean another, not all the time but much of the time. Their thoughts often do not match the spoken word. This ability, if you can call it that, has bedevilled their progress over millennia," said Researcher Soa.

Chapter 3

Joel lay in bed. Michael was snoring beside him as was his wont. His mind was racing and sleep was impossible. In his mind he moved around the Annunaki spaceship watching them as they worked. Work to them was accessing information from Earth, which they found a very slow process, and discussing the results between them. There was no need to record anything as, if one knew, they all knew. He knew that he didn't have their level of clarity of thought and the understanding they had between themselves but each day his thoughts became clearer.

"Joel, this is Belinda," he heard.

"Hi, Belinda," he thought as if he was having a normal conversation. "I sensed your presence at the Maximilian Browne presentation."

"And I yours, but I hadn't developed the skills to communicate. It comes in time though," she thought. "There is another like us, a woman from Italy. Her name is Alessandra D'Angelo. I can only sense her weekly but she is like us, I feel sure of that," she thought.

"Then perhaps her skill is only just becoming apparent. I will reach out when we have finished to try and reach her," thought Joel.

"I need to meet you," thought Belinda.

"And I you. I feel many telepaths go their entire life without meeting but I cannot see that being our way," thought Joel.

"No, it is too ingrained in our psyche to want to meet," thought Belinda. Joel could sense her underlying excitement at being able to discuss telepathically. "I am staying in a dive in Chicago hoping I could make contact. There's a Starbucks down the street near Crown Fountain."

"I know it, 10.00 tomorrow," thought Joel.

"I sensed you traveling through the Annunaki ship. I can't wait to be able to do that," said Belinda as her thoughts vanished slowly into the ether.

Joel lay back down and stared into the blackness that was the ceiling. The blackout curtains that Michael had insisted on kept out all the light and let in little sound. As he concentrated, he could hear the odd automobile but nothing else. Then the thoughts of Alessandra D'Angelo started to come into his head. They were weak and frightened at something she didn't understand. "I am Joel from America and also can hear the Annunaki," he thought. Then nothing.

The following morning her had just sat back down with the coffees a Belinda entered.

"Over here," he thought.

She looked in his direction and moved toward him.

"A really, really, milky coffee," he thought.

"How did you know," she thought and they laughed together but whether they laughed telepathically or out loud neither of them knew.

"It's good to meet you," said Belinda.

"And you. I thought I was going mad only a few short days ago, but now I see things much clearer," said Joel.

"Me too, I couldn't understand what was happening to me but gradually it became clear," said Belinda. "Now I am so excited. Well, excited and fearful I suppose. Excited at being part of it and fearful of what the Annunaki intend," she said.

"They are deciding on the future of the human race," thought Joel rather than speak.

"That is pretty profound," though Belinda. Joel realized that when she thought she had no New York accent.

"Joel, Belinda, came a thought."

"It's Alessandra, can you hear me" she thought.

"We can both hear you," thought Joel as he sipped his coffee.

"I have been listening to your thoughts. I have gone through the same doubts as you, but now I understand. I am no longer frightened. There are others, I can sense them but their telepathic powers are just awakening," thought Alessandra.

"You are Italian?' thought Belinda.

"Yes, and you are American," thought Alessandra. "There is no language barrier I understand you perfectly. I can picture your apartment in New York and even Toby, your little Dachshund. I know you as you know me."

"You are an environmentalist?" thought Joel.

"Yes, I work in the fields of deforestation and conservation and I have my own show on the Internet and a large following," thought Alessandra.

"The Annunaki are aware of that," thought Joel. "They are hoping you can use your celebrity to help them."

"I haven't picked that up on that yet. You are my only telepath contacts so far and unlike you I have not been able to reach the Annunaki on Mars with my thoughts," thought Alessandra.

"It takes a little time," thought Joel as Alessandra faded away.

"Let's get two more coffees," said Belinda. "I want to stay here all day. I have so much to learn."

"An Americano for you and a really, really, milky coffee for me," she said when she returned. "I know I am a bit younger than you but I recognize that this is serious. The Annunaki are going to decide on the future of mankind and we need to help them make the right decision," said Belinda.

"And what is the right decision?" asked Joel.

****

"So, Clyde, now that all the fuss has died down, what do you really think happened to the New Horizons probe?" asked Jenny.

"I don't know, I can't make any sense of it at all. It defies Newton's first law of motion and that is inviolate. Unless Newton got it wrong the only possibility is that our probe was acted on by an outside force," said Clyde.

"And being Devil's Advocate what outside force could that be?" asked Jenny.

"To quote from Sherlock Holmes when asked by the London detective in 'Silver Blaze' if there was anything else, he wished to draw to his attention, he replied 'To the curious incident of the dog in the night time.' In the story the dog didn't bark. The point really is to look at what is missing that should be there. Holmes was famous for saying 'When you have eliminated the impossible, whatever remains, however impossible must be the truth?' "

"So, apart from being well-read," said Jenny with a grimace on her face. "What is your point?"

"I cannot accept that Newton got it wrong. If he did everything we have been doing at NASA and in the world at large is wrong. The probe may have passed through a gateway into another dimension only to emerge at the same spot and still heading on the same course and same speed as has been speculated but that requires an unknown gateway to be present and an odds defying possibility that the probe emerged at the same point and traveling at the same speed and trajectory. I think the odds of that scenario is miniscule to the point of being worth ignoring."

"So, what happened?" she asked.

"If you quote me on this, I will put sugar in your coffee, do you understand?" he replied.

45

"I think that for the first time in my lifetime that FOX News got it right. As the man said 'Aliens'. As far as I can see, and using my Sherlock Holmes logic when you have eliminated the impossible, whatever remains, however impossible must be the truth? The only logical answer was that the probe was taken on board by the aliens, probably the Annunaki as they seem to be all over social media these days and released after examination on the same trajectory and at the same speed. Only the aliens would have the technology to accomplish that. There is no other answer that meets all of the known facts. It answers the missing three months and it answers the continuation of the course and speed," said Clyde.

"You are genuinely saying that you believe that aliens intercepted the New Horizons probe?" asked Jenny.

"Between the two of us and only in this room, yes," answered Clyde.

"Thank God!" exclaimed Jenny. "I thought everyone would think me mad if I said what I thought out loud. Now there are at least two of us who are mad. So, humour me, the aliens intercepted New Horizons in order to examine it and to see the state of our advanced technology. Why?"

"Because they are curious?" answered Clyde.

"Why?" asked Jenny. "To them we are an undeveloped civilization who can offer them little."

"Because they are returning and want to assess how far we have advanced," said Clyde.

"Very good answer young man. That means that they have been here before," said Jenny.

"Well President Obama did announce the existence of aliens only a few years ago," said Clyde.

"So, who are these aliens?" asked Jenny.

"Obviously, the Annunaki. As we all know from the film, they are due to return in 2022, three years from now. No seriously look at it; the film, the books and the news reports. No one cared about the Annunaki ten years ago, they were myth and legend, nothing else. Now Maximilian Browne is on your T.V. screen every night, his books are selling like hot-cakes, and he is on a world tour. There must be more to it than coincidence," said Clyde.

"So, the Annunaki have read the prophesies and are coming back in three years' time?" asked Jenny.

"Yep, you've got it," said Clyde. "They are a punctual race."

"Stop kidding about. What if they come back on regular intervals to check on us? What if it was the Annunaki who implanted this alien DNA that we here so much about in us?"

"Then I think they would be pretty disappointed with what their genetic engineering has turned out. Look at us, billions of us slowly destroying the planet. I wouldn't be too impressed," said Clyde.

"The trouble is Clyde that I believe everything you say. It may not be the Annunaki, it could be any of a number of alien species from what President Obama revealed, but the fact remains that the probe was intercepted and then released at the same speed and on the same trajectory. Only an alien race would have the technology and the ability to do that," said Jenny.

"So, what do you suggest?" asked Clyde.

"We have the resources of NASA to hand, I suggest we go and find them if they are still in the solar system," said Jenny.

"And where do you think we should start looking?" asked Clyde.

"Mars," replied Jenny.

"Why Mars?" asked Clyde.

"Would you like to be cooped up on an intergalactic spaceship for three long years?" asked Jenny.

"And what will they be doing for those three long years?" asked Clyde.

"Looking at us," said Jenny. "Looking at us."

****

"Have you completed your evaluations of the human specimens," thought Captain Mir.

"It has been an interesting, although often conflicting experience for both me and Researcher Zal, but we have finished this phase of the evaluation of the species," thought Researcher Soa.

"I have monitored you as you would expect but would like to hear both of your thoughts on the matter," thought Captain Mir.

"There were many points we considered but the one that stood out was the diversity of the humans. Their diversity in the way they think, the way they view the world, and the way in which they interact with each other," thought Researcher Soa.

"Their thought process varies considerably. Unlike our species there is often a considerable difference in their intellectual capability which seems to be linked to attributable factors such as their parents and ancestors, although those of lesser intellectual capability can advance within their society if they have a better education. We found evidence in some of the specimens that some of equal intellect did better than others due to the effort put into their education," thought Researcher Zal.

"This is where those with more of their money have an advantage as their parents can pay for a better education. Their school systems are very hierarchical and status driven. It seems to be the case that those of similar intellect and intelligence at birth can improve their situation by buying a better education," thought Researcher Soa.

"Their education system differs from our approach in that we are able to test for the skills of individual at birth and from that can define what path they should follow. It also differs in that education is very competitive, in fact the species as a whole is very competitive," thought Researcher Zal. "It was interesting that one specimen did not value his education highly and now lives on the margins of society whereas others who were well-educated seem to fare much better.

"The competitive nature of their society plays a major part in what drives them. They seem to seek to want to excel at whatever they chose to do, be it sport, work, music or writing. Not all succeed and their failure often blights their life. Competition does not only drive individuals but it drives their nations. Some look back toward a glorious but faded past while others look forward to a future than lifts them out of their current state and into the future. Those countries whose dominance is fading have, particularly in recent years, looked inward and in doing so have fallen prey to opportunists who have pushed their own agenda which is at odds to good government," thought Researcher Zal."

"I have seen that unlike us they have no ruling council that makes decisions globally," thought Captain Mir.

"There are organizations who operate on a global level but they are often kept short of funds or dismissed in the media as favouring one country above others. The human reliance on nation states makes them appear petty and self-interested, but to me the biggest losers of the nation state are those that sit at the bottom, many of those are in the continent they call Africa. Their children often starve or become ill through lack of clean water and sanitation while the richer nations spend their wealth on trivial purchases. Many, but not all, seem oblivious to the inequality on their planet," thought Researcher Zal.

"There is a trait of self-interest that ran through all the specimens we examined to a lesser or greater degree. This is not part of our culture as we are open between ourselves, as telepaths perhaps we have evolved that way but I found it unsettling. We work for the collective good of our species while many of the sample group we examined work only for the good of themselves and their immediate family. Very little outside that seems to matter," thought Researcher Soa.

"Having said that two of the samples returned offered a refreshing insight into the humans. One, a man of religion, a Buddhist, who maintained his family while supporting those less advantaged in his community, and one who had left her home country to work with the poor in Africa. Overall, we found then difficult to categorize. As a species they are capable of a high level of indifference toward others, while others care about their fellow humans to a degree that exceeds ours. They are capable of extreme cruelty and of an abundance of kindness. They remain an enigma to me," thought Researcher Zal.

"We have three years until our return in 2022. Researcher Soa you are to form new teams to examine the humans more closely. From our short session here, we need to examine the role of money in their societies, the importance of the nation state to them and their politics which appear very short-term and prone to opportunism, and any other areas that you feel pertain to us gaining an in-depth knowledge of this species," thought Captain Mir.

"Researcher Aom and Researcher Yan are examining their religions and the planets environmental issues respectively. Myself and Researcher Zal will integrate our research with theirs. They are a complex species and all these factors appear to overlap to make them what they are," thought Researcher Soa.

****

Badr El-Din fought the demons in his head. The voices, however, became clearer every day. He prayed to the prophet Mohammed that they be gone but still the voices persisted. He could hear European voices as they talked. He understood what they were saying but they were the words of the infidel.

"The Prophet Mohammed is the one true God," he repeated to himself over and over again but still the voices in his head persisted. As his mind began to open, he would slam it closed. Without sleep for four agonizing days, he was found by his friend Ahmad who concerned about not seeing him bribed a guard to open the cell door.

"He has gone mad," said the guard. "I must lock the door. The evil within him must not escape."

"No, please let me take him out into the courtyard and clean him. If you leave him here, he will die," said Ahmad.

"I will not touch him," said the guard.

Ahmad tugged and pulled Badr's skinny body toward the light. As the light hit his eyes, he let out a piercing scream before retreating back into his mind and finding solace in his chant. The guard left and Ahmad tended to the now still body of his friend, both of them, locked in this hell-hole for over ten years. He gave him water and bathed him.

It is his time to die, thought Ahmad to himself but Badr did not die. Instead, as he regained his strength and fought the demons in his head. He vowed to escape his prison and silence the noises in his head. It was his obligation to the Prophet Mohammed.

Chapter 4

"You are telling me that you are hearing voices?" asked her manager Steffano Icardi.

"No, I'm telling you that I am a telepath, and that I am able to communicate with other telepaths," said Alessandra. "In fact, I am telling you a lot more than that I you don't think I'm mad."

"And where did the gift come from?" asked a highly sceptical Steffano.

"The Annunaki," replied Alessandra.

"The Annunaki?" said Steffano. "Like in the film?"

"Not exactly, the film is nothing like the true Annunaki," said Alessandra.

"Of course, it isn't," said the increasingly cynical Steffano.

"Okay, I'll lay it out for you and you can decide for yourself. If you think I have suddenly gone mad I wouldn't blame you but hear me out," she said.

Steffano signalled to the waiter for two more cold beers.

"Go ahead," he said.

"A week ago, I wasn't a telepath and life was normal. Now I am in communication with two other telepaths in America and others are beginning to recognize and come to terms with their gift. The Annunaki have remained in orbit around our sun in the Pluto-Charon system until last week when they moved in to establish a base on Mars. As they did so their presence has awakened the latent capability of those who retain the telepathic powers since the Annunaki altered the DNA of early humans over fourteen million years ago. They have come here to assess both the planet and our stewardship of it," said Alessandra.

"Then they are going to be very disappointed," said Steffano.

"That's the point," said Alessandra. "They are due to make themselves known in the year 2022. We have three years in which to demonstrate that man is able to heal the planet."

"And if we can't?" asked Steffano.

"Then they will be forced to make a decision about the future of mankind," said Alessandra. "To their way of thinking the planet is more important than us humans. We can be replaced, the planet cannot."

Steffano sat in silence as he thought about what he had just been told.

"I have known you for many years and your commitment to the environment has been unwavering. Together we have built you in an international celebrity with nearly ten million followers across the globe. I presume your intention is to use your status to spread the message you have just told me?" he asked.

"As you say you have known me for many years. That is exactly what I intend," she said.

"And you want me to support you and carry on managing you?" he asked.

"Exactly," she said.

"Of course, I will. No one could come up with that story unless it were true or they were barking mad. I know you can be a little headstrong but I've never equated it to madness. What is it you want me to do?" Steffano asked.

"Nothing stupid. It's taken years to build up my credibility. We will challenge the world to achieve meaningful and measurable improvements in three years by the year 2022. No mention of the Annunaki, no mention of telepathy, just a three-year challenge instead of the usual 2050 tipping-point date.

"Brilliant!" he laughed. "I can see you've thought this thought."

"Yes, a global challenge. If I can get the momentum behind us, and I know I can then we can make the world sit up and listen," said Alessandra.

"And why are you so certain?" asked Steffano.

"Because I will soon have many more telepathic contacts who will spread the world and, more than that, time will pass and the aura of the Annunaki being so close will be increasingly noticed. You can see it already if you look around you, the film a worldwide blockbuster, books, magazines, Facebook – the Annunaki are everywhere and this is only the start. We have three years until the arrive and we cannot afford to waste it. We must convince them we can save the planet," said Alessandra.

"Why?" asked Steffano.

"Because we must," said Alessandra.

"I'll trust you; you wouldn't be embarking on a course of action as mad as this without a reason, I also know you wouldn't have come here empty handed," said Steffano.

Alessandra took out her phone and accessed their website.

"These are not published, of course, but they outline the campaign I have in mind," said Alessandra.

"Two more cold beers," said Steffano.

****

It was as if the voices from the past had come back to haunt him

Ahmad was held in a small six foot by six-foot cell. Light came in through a grate in the ceiling. If he was lucky the guards would allow him to wash once a week but they often forgot. One day they would come and take him out to the courtyard to be either shot or garrotted. He would prefer to be shot; he had had a long time to think about it.

"Ahmed, can you hear me," came a thought. He looked around to see where the voice had come from. "Ahmad, can you hear me. It's me Badr."

"I can hear you," said Ahmad. "What ....." but before he could continue Badr's voice returned.

"Tell the guard you think I might be dead. Tell him I have not knocked on the wall for three days," thought Badr.

"You go in first," said the guard pointing at Badr's body lying on the floor. "If he's dead you can be the one to see. I hate the dead."

As Ahmad leaned over him Badr passed him a three-inch shank made of bone. Ahmad knew what he was being asked to do. He stood up and turned to the guard and in one movement the shank ran down his neck. With his eyes wide open the guard gargled his last breath and then quietly fell to the floor supported by Badr and Ahmed.

Ahmad followed Badr as he turned right and they moved carefully down the passageway to where another guard sat. Badr took the shank from Ahmed and crept up behind him. He slumped over his desk as the blood flowed into the open draw. Badr took his gun and Ahmed took the keys. It was as if Badr knew where everyone was. Ahmad would realize later that he could sense people but then he just followed Badr's lead. They hid in the back of a cart which wasn't even checked as they went through the main gate. They were free.

"This house is empty," thought Badr.

Ahmad didn't realize that Badr wasn't talking. The door was opened and they went inside.

"Get some clothes, these one's stink. We can wash by the river. I'll see if they have any money," thought Badr. They washed and changed under the cover of some date trees and with a tidy sum of money in their pockets flagged down a passing truck. Within three hours they were both one of many in the bustling streets of Damascus.

Badr talked and prayed with people. Ahmed looked on as first a few people attached themselves to him and within a few days the number exceeded one hundred. Badr held them in the palm of his hand. He talked of the Prophet and he talked of the past. He went back in time to the founders of this land. Imperceptibly, as his flock continued to grow, he raged against those he called "the thinkers." It was as if he had struck a chord as something deep inside people's memories stirred. The thinkers were not welcome.

****

Maximilian Browne was worried. The voices in his head were getting louder and were telling him things about the Annunaki that made no sense to him. Born William Cant, he had served ten years for fraud and burglary before embarking on his career as the world's leading authority on the Annunaki. He had always liked their stories and they manner in which they challenged the Old Testament. He used to rile his bible-bashing father something rotten in the old days by quoting from The Story of Gilgamesh.

"Max, we need to get a move on. The plane leaves in a couple of hours and we are due in Denver tonight, from what they tell me we are a sell-out," said DeVane, his confidante, lover and manager. "There is no doubt that when good old President Obama admitted to the existence of aliens, he gave our business a mighty lift," she added.

"There's more to it than that. Look at the film and look at my book sales, there is genuine interest in the Annunaki now," said Maximilian as he snapped his suitcase shut.

"Long may it continue, honey," said DeVane.

"There's something niggling me though," he said.

"What's that?" asked DeVane.

"They're back," Max replied.

"Who?"

"The Annunaki."

"The Annunaki?"

"DeVane, I think the legends are true and they are returning in 2022," said Maximilian.

"Yea, right."

"No, listen to me. I hear their voices very night. It's like they are trying to talk with me, but it is all very distant," said Maximilian.

"Keep that to yourself d'you here me. We have found the golden egg and I, for one, want to maximize our return on it. Stick to the script, you know it backwards but leave this 'they're back' stuff well out of it."

****

The mother ship deviated from its projected return path to Niburu.

"Planet X43-943-Ab is within sensor range," thought navigator Lim. "Initial readings show an increase in carbon in their atmosphere, but other readings are similar to our last survey."

"Who undertook the last survey?" thought the Commodore.

"That was Commodore Plin two journeys ago. He did not visit the planet but carried out a class 3 survey as we have just done," thought navigator Lim.

"The increase in carbon in their atmosphere could be the first sign of a civilization. Alter course we need to take a closer look," thought the captain.

"The planet is aflame," said navigator Lim. "Its outer atmosphere is being stripped away by its sun and the planet has dried out. The vegetation on its surface has caught fire and engulfed the planet in a global fireball. Life may be sheltering underground, but it will emerge to a dying world," thought navigator Lim.

"Resume course," thought the Commodore.

"Got ya'," thought navigator Lim.

The Commodore when into the thought booth. This unit enabled person-to-person thought communication but was restricted to senior officers only.

"He thought 'got ya', thought the Commodore.

"Navigator Lim? He is always precise in his thoughts," thought Captain Mir.

"It worries me as this is the first sign that the humans may have infected the crew with their behaviours," thought the Commodore.

"And you will be journeying across the cosmos for eons," though Captain Mir.

"I have put as many of the crew into stasis as I can, but who knows the situation when they wake," thought the Commodore. "Do you have any unexplained infections apparent in your crew yet?"

"My crew is functioning correctly," thought Captain Mir.

"That is good to know. Be watchful and keep me updated," thought the Commodore.

****

"You have been studying their history," thought Captain Mir. "What conclusions have you drawn?"

"In truth, it's difficult to draw conclusions," thought Researcher Lao. "There are patterns, but the humans are highly unpredictable and easily swayed. After the early civilizations the Chinese were one of the first empires to dominate a region over an extended time-frame, but the rise and downfall of their empires gives us an insight into the humans. Their empires would rise through war, have a period of flowering, tax to heavily, become corrupt, and then the populace would revolt against them. In simple terms that is what happened time and time again. A new Emperor would be proclaimed only to follow the same path. In the case of China, the empire remained while the ruling elite changed until time and events caught up with them and the empire was no more."

"It is a pattern you see time and time again. Empires would often go through an expansionist period when they held an advantage against others. The British, a warlike race from the northern hemisphere forged the first global Empire with a blend of piracy, cruelty, and military superiority, at one point they ruled half of the known world. To maintain their empire, like all empires, they had to continually expand. When their expansion stopped, they went the way of the Romans, the Persians and other great empires of their past and withdrew into themselves, something that is still going on today nearly a century after their golden era," thought Researcher Qim.

"What do you mean by 'withdrawing into themselves?'" questioned Captain Mir.

"They are a nation that consider themselves as superior to others, whereas as now they are, in global terms, just another country. Their unique history, their former world domination and their heroes all serve to define and enhance the opinion they have of themselves," thought Researcher Qim.

"It is not only true of Great Britain but the same could be said of the United States of America, China, Germany, France and many others. The issue that has often raised its head is how a nation's history is written. It is often a far cry from the truth. Defeat is embellished as victory, lost battles become winning battles and massacres become skirmishes. 'It's the winners who write the history,' to quote an American Indian Chief called Black Fox," continued Researcher Qim.

"I have trouble understanding this national identity?" thought Captain Mir.

"Take us as an example. Besides our physical make-up what makes us Annunaki?" thought Researcher Qim.

"Our history, our deeds, our great scientists and explorers, our love for one another," thought Captain Mir.

"It is all that and more for the humans, but they look not only at a people as a whole, they look at their small segment of it. They divide the world, nation against nation, black against white, rich against poor and, looking at what is happening on the planet at the moment many nations are on the verge of becoming dysfunctional as they divide themselves with their particular understanding of the truth," thought Researcher Qim.

"However, this is not true in many cases," thought Researcher Lao. "There are many people who, throughout their entire history have cared for others, be it next to a soldier on the battlefield, or be it after they have been wounded, or be it when they are old. Some people seem able to place the needs of individuals above that of their country and above their own personal needs. It is something we see time and time again and is one of the most impressive of all the human traits."

"These are the people we need to encourage. Those who can look beyond their narrow confines and view the good of the world as paramount. I am still waiting for an analysis on religion, the environment and the current political situation, but from the thoughts of yourself and the others I sense a pattern emerging. A generalization but there are those who want a better, fairer future for both themselves and the planet and those who are narrow-minded and focused on events as they are now. This doesn't appear to be in just the leading countries but across the globe. If we are to save both this planet and this dominant species then we need to facilitate a major shift in thinking and, at the moment I can only think of one way of achieving that and I am disciplined by training not to allow that thought to enter my head," thought Captain Mir.

"I need to know more about the humans, both good and bad. Our first concern is the continuance of the planet and ensuring it is habitable. Whether that will be for humans we have time to find out, but I look at their disrespect for their planet with concern. I hear the thoughts of all those in the crew as they continue the research and wonder if there is the will amongst the humans to view their planet as what it is, a jewel among planets," the captain continued.

"This is the only planet they know; they do not appreciate how their planet is so unique," thought Researcher Lao.

"They have an understanding. Their astronomy is backward by our standards, but they are aware of the formation process of their solar system, of why the planets within it are as they are and they have looked at distant planets and realized how few are habitable. They have treaties to limit the poisons that they emit into their atmosphere, but appear to ignore them. As a race they seem to put their immediate needs ahead of those of the planet. The earth will heal itself if given time, but that time may only be possible if the humans were no longer on the planet.

Chapter 5

In his mind he was in the city of Ur, Sumeria in the year 4,200 B.C. The great king Eridug had just been entombed with his most loyal followers, those who had earned the honour of being permitted to die alongside their king. He could sense others around him who had the gift and he struggled to keep his mind closed. He used his influence and money to buy an audience with the new king, King Emenluana. His senses told him that King Emenluana did not have the gift, the first king of Ur not to have it. He understood that the new king wanted the 'thinkers' gone from his kingdom, or from the face of the Earth.

"And what is it you wish of me?" asked the young king only fourteen years of age.

"I am Badr of Damascus and I wish to rid the kingdom of thinkers," he said.

"Damascus, this is not a city that I have heard of," replied the king. "Badr of Damascus you are a thinker are you not?"

"I am, much to my shame, and in coming before you today my life is forfeit. I do not ask you to spare my life, I ask that you permit me to use my sense to root out this evil of thought that bedevils your kingdom. When my work is done, I will present myself to you to do with me what you wish," said Badr.

He opened his eyes and was in the present. His dream, if that is what it was, was so clear. He could still smell the pure air and the tang of fresh fruit that drifted through the palace of Ur. Badr closed his eyes to remember every detail as he vainly tried to sleep and return to this other world he had just visited.

"I will honour my obligation to King Emenluana even if it costs me my life," thought Badr El-Din.

****

Researcher Zal opened her eyes wide. She had heard the threat but it was weak.

"There is a threat to thinkers on Planet Earth," she thought. "The message is feint and originates from a newly awakened telepath."

Researcher Soa looked at her, bidding her to concentrate.

"It is from a time long ago, and also from the present. The thought is confused as if the telepath himself is struggling," thought Researcher Zal.

"It is a man," thought Researcher Soa.

"Yes. He has gone to a past time, a time that saw the commencement of bloody persecution against thinkers," thought Researcher Zal.

"Persecution, that explains why there are so few thinkers left," thought Researcher Soa.

"I can sense from him that he was in the city of Ur. A city at the beginning of their civilization. He was involved in much killing before he met his end," thought Researcher Zal.

"And he lives again" thought Researcher Zal. "This cannot be."

"Our telepath is from the present but his mind has journeyed back eons. The early need to eliminate our brothers and sisters must have been very strong as their civilization developed."

"He must be eliminated," thought Captain Mir from another part of the spaceship.

"Would it not be better to learn from him," thought Researcher Zal. "I have established the link and can monitor his actions. It would be useful to learn of the early times and the deaths of our brothers and sisters. To learn from the past, you must first understand the past."

"You are correct," thought Captain Mir. "Monitor him closely, to traverse time in this manner his need to kill telepaths must be very strong. It is important that those telepaths we have established communication with remain alive. Their role in communicating between us and the humans will increase as we near our return."

"I understand," thought Researcher Zal.

****

Alessandra sat at her keyboard hoping that she was putting the final touches to her campaign. The problem was her manager Steffano, a perfectionist in every sense of the word.

"The red is not right," he said. "We need it a shade darker or maybe a little more crimson in colour. That's it. Now we are looking good for our launch. You have a series of interviews, both online and on television tomorrow. Here are the scripts we agreed. I know you understand the three-year campaign better than I do but it never hurts to be over prepared."

"Yes, that colour does look better," said Alessandra. "I will just proofread the text one more time and then call it a day."

"I'm meeting with Jorge Kackimarcik at Zero One for a final briefing," he said.

"And a beer or two," interject Alessandra.

"Probably, but don't work too late, it's a big day tomorrow," he said as he left.

Alessandra put her glasses back on and returned for her final proofread. She was half-an-hour in when she became aware of a voice in her head.

"Alessandra, I am Researcher Zal, please don't be frightened," thought Researcher Zal.

"Researcher Zal," said Alessandra.

"No need to talk we are both telepaths," thought Researcher Zal. "I have been watching your progress with interest. One of our major concerns is the state of your planet and the way in which humans abuse it."

"You echo my thoughts, as I feel sure you know," thought Alessandra.

"Tomorrow is a big day for you with the launch of your three-year initiative in order to make a meaningful difference to the planet," thought Researcher Zal.

"You thought 'the' planet and not 'your' planet," thought Alessandra picking up on Researcher Zal's thoughts immediately.

"That is one of the issues with telepathy. You are now linked with me subconsciously and you will start to read my mind if only to a limited degree. You will soon realize that we are here not only to evaluate you as the species we chose to dominate this planet, but to see if we allow you to continue as the dominant species. To us it is the planet that we consider above anything else," thought Researcher Zal.

"And you think we are abusing it," thought Alessandra.

"We have travelled the cosmos for millions of years. Humans do not understand the riches they have been given with a planet such as Earth. Our planet is dull and barren by comparison, but you humans seem on a path where life may find it difficult to survive and that point may come sooner than many humans expect," thought Researcher Zal. "We cannot allow such a wondrous planet to die. We elevated your ancestors in the dim and distant past and if we find that you have proven yourselves unworthy of our decision then we will terminate humans from the planet."

"You can do that?" thought Alessandra.

"In the blink of an eye, not that we blink, of course" thought Researcher Zal as she made her first ever joke.

"I know you understand not to mention us or our presence. Be assured we will visit your planet in 2022 and we are researching all aspects of your civilization to ensure we arrive at the correct decision," thought Researcher Zal.

"And I can tell from your thoughts that you haven't reached a decision yet," thought Alessandra.

"That is not our way. We will decide in three years from now," thought Researcher Zal. "I contacted you first as your launch is tomorrow. I will contact Joel and Belinda shortly."

"You are hiding something?" thought Alessandra.

"Yes, there is another telepath who we have concerns about. He is unimportant at this time," thought Researcher Zal. "Tomorrow your launch will be maximized on all your media channels. I will ensure that. To us, manipulating your computer systems is easy. What you are proposing with your message of three-years to clean up the planet is important. More important than perhaps you were aware of."

"I never realized how important until we had this discussion," thought Alessandra.

****

"We first made physical contact with this planet over fourteen million of their years ago," thought Researcher Aom. "Our team carried out a rigorous selection process before deciding that a developing species now known as hominids should have their DNA modified in such a way that would both enhance their brain development and permit telepathic speech. Over many millions of years, the hominids developed into the forefathers of the race we see on the planet today".

"From the result we see in present day humans that the DNA enhancement did not work as planned?" thought Captain Mir.

"No, looking back our Researchers were too successful in many ways. In choosing hominids they inadvertently chose the species that probably would have come to dominate the planet without their involvement. Their enhancement of the brain function passed throughout the species over time, but the ability for telepathic communication not only faded by being diluted, but became the first major divide between the species. A considerable amount of effort was put in by those who communicated by speech to eliminate those they called the 'thinkers,' particularly in the period when the species progressed from being hunter-gatherers into developing an agricultural society. As hunter-gathers the 'thinkers' would pass unnoticed but as the population grew and enclosed itself with settlements the trait of thinking became more obvious, and those who did not have the ability increasingly sought to eradicate it," thought Researcher Aom,

"The past has left thought traces in the humans so it easier to understand the events of millions of years ago. The power of telepathy still exists in a miniscule number of the population today, as does the hatred of telepaths. We are already sensing this from one individual on the planet, but it is currently lying dormant in many more as far as the team can tell," thought Researcher Aom. "What we have also discovered is that the memory of the early Annunaki, most likely enhanced by our return visits has imprinted an image of us in the minds of the humans, an image that exists to this day."

"That our early visits remained in their memory is surprising," thought Captain Mir.

"It went further than that. Over time they came to worship the memory and build a god-like narrative around it. Too those early civilizations we were worshipped as Gods," thought Researcher Aom.

"This concept of a God is an area I struggle with," thought Captain Mir.

"I too struggled, but I can see the answer in the differences between ourselves and the humans. To compare the two species one aspect stands out, that the average human has an I.Q of one hundred, whereas ours averages two hundred and fifty on their scale of measurement.

"We understood very early in our development the makeup of the heavens but, to early man it was a mystery, as were the floods, drought, and the pestilence that often raged over their land. They sought solace and found it initially in the worship of the heavens and in the worship of us. Over time tales were told and stories embellished until they became regarded as factual and recorded as writing developed," thought Researcher Aom.

"We worship no God or Gods as we had no need. We understood the events surrounding us, and they did not. That is a very interesting observation," thought Captain Mir.

"We, the Annunaki, faded from their collective consciousness, but not before some of the early civilizations recorded their rather enhanced interpretation of us. Over time we were replaced by other gods, although our proximity in their solar system seems to have reignited the humans' interest in us," thought Researcher Aom.

"And their current religions?" thought Captain Mir.

"They have many of which Christianity is the largest and Islam the second. A full report has been prepared, but it is lengthy and detailed. Religion has played an important role and development of the humans. The report has been loaded on your stasis pod so you can listen as you sleep. Our analysis, particularly over recent years has seen two marked trends in the major religions. One is a marked move to the basic fundamentals of each religion, and this is as true of the Christian faith as well as the Muslim faith. This shift in thinking has brought much unrest between the dominant religions. The other trend is a move away from religion. As the sciences reveal the truth of the birth of the universe many find it difficult to reconcile what is scientific fact with what they increasingly perceive as the superstitions of the past," thought Researcher Aom.

"Wars have been waged in the name of their religions both against each other and within their respective religions. The faith and belief that these humans can have in their religion can be exceptionally strong. All religions forbid killing but it runs through most religions like a thread," thought Researcher Aom as she continued her thought process.

"Do these religions establish the precepts that humans should adhere to within their particular religions?" thought Captain Mir.

"Religions establish codes of behaviour that the adherents are supposed to follow?" said Researcher Aom.

"Supposed to?" thought captain Mir.

"We are fortunate from our viewpoint. As telepaths we can understand the minds of these humans better than they can themselves. I say 'supposed to' deliberately. The humans of all religions often flout them, often in thought and less frequently in deed. They seem to put considerable weight on "the word of God," or however it is prescribed in their religion, but often pay little more than lip-service to these edicts in their daily lives," thought Researcher Aom.

"Their history is riddled with examples where acts of unspeakable barbarity have been carried out in the name of their respective God, or in the early years Gods," continued Researcher Aom.

"And your opinion?" thought Captain Mir

"Religion serves it purpose in establishing social order, patterns of behaviour, and in giving adherents faith in something. That seems to be important to humans. It is clear that, as the civilization progresses, more and more of the humans are casting doubt on religion. Not all believe and that has become more obvious as their science advances and their society becomes more questioning. The concept of an over-arching God has difficulty when presented with the scientific discoveries they have made, particularly in archaeology, genetics, and astronomy," thought Researcher Aom.

"And the announcement of their President Obama of the existence of aliens?" thought Captain Mir.

"That has enlivened the debate, spawned more of what the humans call 'conspiracy theories,' and has opened the door for opportunists to build huge religious following based on their beliefs," thought Researcher Aom.

"Including Maximilian Browne and his tall tales about us," thought Captain Mir.

"He is just one among many," thought Researcher Aom. "Many new cults built on the personality of one man have arisen. They are in most cases nothing more than opportunists, or those with a distorted view that draws adherents to them. The knowledge of the existence of aliens has forced the religions to look outside their earth-centric view and incorporate a wider, more powerful God who created not only the earth, but the cosmos," thought Researcher Aom.

"An admission on such a scale must have shaken these religions to the core," thought Captain Mir.

"They are all incorporating the existence of aliens into their narrative, although to many there is now even more reason to be sceptical of religion," thought Researcher Aom.

****

Badr El-Din sat on the back of a donkey cart as people jostled for space around him.

"Sit my brothers and sisters," he said indicating to them with his hands. "I am here to take you far back in time. Back in time to when this land was the cradle of civilization. Back to the city of Ur, a magnificent kingdom to the east, but not one without its problems. I was honoured with an audience with King Emenluana who came to the throne at a young age."

His eyes appeared to glaze over as he spoke and slowly, he entered a deep, almost catatonic state.

"The young king was the first ruler of Ur who did not have the curse of telepathy, the ability to communicate using only the power of your mind. Those with this curse could plot and scheme with secret and malignant thoughts between themselves. Their curse had bedevilled the human race since its birth. The new king wanted the thinkers gone from his land, not only gone but dead," he said as he started to slowly sway back and forth, eyes open and showing only the white, on the tail of the donkey cart. All before him were mesmerized.

"Much to my shame, I carried the curse. I offered to use my curse to find others with the power of thought and to kill them. The young king gave me his blessing and I undertook my quest. My brothers and sisters, this was not an easy undertaking. The 'thinkers' could read my mind, as I could read theirs. It took time but I learned to shield my mind from their probing. when I had control of my curse, I was free to search them out and kill them, and kill them I did. Doing so left me weak and defenceless for many days after as the anger of the thinkers invaded by consciousness, but I fought them over and over again.

"My life was given freely to King Emenluana but it was not he who would take my life. I was searching, searching, trying to hear a thought. I was close and my dagger was readied. I remember the smell of goats as they passed and then I was dead. I do not know by whose hand, or in what manner but all was gone. Now I live again, and still thinkers walk among us. I must complete my oath to King Emenluana, I must rid the world of these people, they're a curse," he said as he went silent. Slowly the swaying stopped, his eyeballs returned and he was in the present.

"I must rid the world of these people," he repeated as if to himself.

Chapter 6

"We have New Horizons working fine and I have programmed in the coordinates that will allow us to take the images of Proxima Centauri and Wolf 359 as we had originally planned, although three months late," said Clyde.

"If it works it will give us a parallax measurement that can be combined with Earth-based images to determine the exact distance to these stars," said Jenny.

Bill Manners, his coffee in his hand entered the room.

"This is the only room apart from my office where I can drink a coffee," he said.

"Well keep the cup away from my computers," replied Clyde. "If you weren't the boss, I would remind you of the office protocols."

"How's the programming going?" Bill asked.

"I am glad to say that it is complete. Now it's just a question of waiting patiently," said Clyde. "Jenny had to re-enter all the data sets from scratch. It took her an eternity."

"Boss, there's something we want your opinion on," continued Clyde a bit sheepishly.

"Go ahead," said Bill.

"Well here goes," started Jenny. "We have looked long and hard at all the theories of the missing three months and finally reached a conclusion."

Bill nodded encouraging her to continue.

"Bear with me on this, it's going to sound pretty far-fetched. Newton's first law of motion states that an object at rest stays at rest and an object in motion stays in motion with the same speed and in the same direction unless acted on by an unbalanced force. Basically, that objects continue to do what they are doing unless something interferes with them in some way," said Jenny.

"Go on," Bill said.

"Discounting the wormhole theory as it makes no sense, there is nothing that should influence the New Horizon probe. All the forces such as gravity from the sun and the planets have already been factored in when New Horizons disappeared. To appear in the same spot in space and traveling on the same course and speed after three months defies Newton's theory. To use the terminology it is our contention, mine and Clyde's, that our probe was acted on by an unbalanced force."

"I can't disagree with anything you've said so far," said Bill as he drained his coffee.

Jenny looked over at Clyde.

"This is where things get a bit science fictiony, if there is such a term," said Clyde. "It is our contention that the outside force was alien, and not only that, it was the Annunaki."

"I'm not sure I'm with you on that, but carry on," said Bill.

"We have been working on this, in our own time of course," said Clyde. "Jenny and I talked it though and both arrived at the same conclusion – that the unbalanced force could only be of alien origin. Nothing else makes sense. Who or what could have made New Horizon vanish from the tracking radar and reappear three months later not only traveling in its projected course but at the correct velocity? Don't worry there's more....

"We surmised that the Annunaki were positioned on the edge of our solar system which is why they were able to capture it and, we imagine, analyse it. When they moved inwards, they released the probe, said Clyde.

"If you move inward from the Pluto-Charon system where would you stop? Don't forget they are due to return in the year 2022," said Jenny.

"Aw come on guys, that was just like in the Tom Cruise film," said Bill.

"No boss, the date 2022 is in the history books as far back as the Babylonians. Do you really think we would come to you without such an outlandish tale without checking the facts?" asked Jenny.

Bill shrugged.

"If you are coming in from the Pluto – Charon system where would you stop?" asked Jenny.

"Logic would dictate Mars," said Bill. "Why would they stop?"

"Because today is the year 2019 and they are not due until 2022," said Jenny.

"And what are they doing for three years?" asked Bill.

"Checking us out, I reckon," replied Clyde.

"There's more to it," said Jenny. "It was Clyde's idea so I will let him tell it."

"Boss, you think that what we already told you is weird, well here's one for you. We set out to find the location of their spaceship on Mars. Clearly it would be well hidden and difficult to spot with our technology, so I tried a different tack. At one point in every day Internet traffic relating to the Annunaki peaks. If you analyse this you will notice that this only happens when one point on the rotation of Mars faces the Earth. From there I could ascertain the longitude where this phenomenon occurred. Then I had to check along the line of longitude to see if I could find the Annunaki spacecraft," said Clyde.

"And did you?" asked Bill.

"No," said Clyde. "But I did find an anomaly. There is one point along the line of longitude where there is no magnetism."

"And you think that this point is where the Annunaki have landed their spacecraft?" asked Bill.

"Sure do," said Clyde.

"And you Jenny?" asked Bill.

"I agree with Clyde. They know we have probes above the surface of Mars and it makes sense that they would camouflage their vessel. It's just that Clyde has seen through their camouflage," replied Jenny.

"What do you think boss?" asked Clyde.

"I think I need to see your evidence first hand," said Bill. "But in the meantime, not a word to anyone and I mean anyone outside of us three."

"Yes Boss," said Jenny and Clyde in unison.

****

It was the air he first noticed as it was so fresh and clear. Joel opened his eyes and stared around. Belinda lay on a bed next to him. The room was huge with a silver tinge that made him relax. He watched as Belinda opened her eyes. "We're here," he thought. She smiled back.

"Welcome," thought the slim figure of Researcher Zal as she approached the two telepaths from Earth."

"Where are we?" thought Belinda.

"On our spaceship on Mars," thought Researcher Zal.

"Are we really on Mars?" thought Joel.

"Go and look for yourself," thought Researcher Zal.

As Joel moved toward a small window and as he did so the entire wall became like glass. On display was a panoramic vista of the dusty, rock-strewn, ochre landscape of Mars. Belinda joined him and they stood side-by-side looking, just looking. A small sand-devil raised its head in the light Martian atmosphere only to drift away. Joel shook his head in disbelief.

"Join us," thought Researcher Zal.

Three aliens faced them. Their skin had a lilac hue and they wore no clothes, apart from that they looked just like you would have seen in the movies. Three aliens, one a man was slightly larger but, apart from that there was no other way of telling. The two female aliens looked at first sight to be identical but there were differences in their eyes and nostrils. Their mouths were small, but it was the eyes that drew you in. They matched the skin tone but the lilac colour shone from them.

"Surreal, here I am sitting opposite three aliens with Mars as a backdrop," thought Belinda. "Surreal."

"Oh, sorry. I forgot you could real my every thought," she thought.

"In fact, we can't read you every thought, but what we can read or not read depends on ourselves and the entity we are interacting with. We have the ability to filter our lesser or more personal thoughts. If we didn't, we would be swamped by the sheer number of thoughts," thought Researcher Zal.

"We always think of being taken aboard alien spacecraft to be tested upon," thought Joel.

"It is strange how that particular events have remained so strong in your collective consciousness. We empty people's minds before they leave, but it seems that that one event makes such an impact on the human psyche that it remains only to re-enacted in books and films," thought Researcher Soa. "But you are not here to be tested in that way. You are here for an entirely different purpose."

"On your planet we have been able to find only four telepaths with the ability we implanted in the early hominids from this distance. We know now that this low number is due to centuries of persecution particularly when you moved from hunter gatherers to a more settled agrarian society. Please don't misunderstand me, there are many more telepaths on your planet as we can see from social media reaction and the general increase in the Annunaki interest. Their abilities will become more apparent as we near the planet, but you are the ones with exceptional ability," thought Researcher Zal.

"In three years', time we will return to Earth. As I know has been explained to you, we are here to evaluate the species we created but also to examine your husbandry of the planet," thought Captain Mir. "We are fortunate that one of our telepaths is an environmentalist. Alessandra has launched her campaign to save the planet. What she and you are aware of is that she is trying to save not only the planet but also the place of mankind on it. Her campaign has launched very successfully and we will aid her in every way."

"Yes, she was in contact last night, ecstatic over the first few days after the launch. She explained how you had aided her," said Joel.

"We very much want the human race to succeed. You bring a joy to the universe that is lacking. You have taught us much through your history, culture and interaction with each other, but you are destroying so much of your planet at an unsustainable rate. Your planet is outstanding and its survival is paramount. We cannot allow your degradation of the planet to continue," thought Captain Mir. "Your planet is nearing its tipping point."

"As we have enlisted Alessandra to help improve not only the planet but the mindset of humans on environmental issues and we are asking you to help us," thought Researcher Zal.

"Of course," was the collective thought from both Belinda and Joel.

"Do not volunteer to readily what we are about to do will change you both forever," thought Researcher Soa.

"What are our lives when compared to saving humanity," thought Joel. Belinda nodded in agreement. "What are you asking of us?"

"We want you to work with Alessandra and help turn her campaign into an international movement," though Captain Mir.

"I am a dispatcher for a parcel company and Belinda is a marketing assistant," thought Joel.

"We will change you, as Researcher Soa thought. You will not return to Earth as you are now. We will greatly enhance your brains capability and understanding, and plant within it knowledge that you cannot imagine," thought Captain Mir. "You will be fully resourced and work with Alessandra at waking your world up to its shameful environmental performance."

"This will be a huge undertaking. Your world seems unable to break away from its dependence on fossil fuel despite concerted efforts from many environmentalists and scientists. You know all the answers but do not put them into practice," thought Researcher Zal.

"What we are asking you to do goes beyond just the environment. We need you to challenge those in power who disregard the needs of the planet in pursuit of personal gain. Over the last century your politics has led to an entrenchment in thinking, looking back rather than looking forward, looking inward rather than outward and looking at self-enrichment at the expense of the planet," thought Researcher Soa.

"And viewing your world from a nationalistic rather than global perspective," added Captain Mir

"We will give you the tools help you to do this, but your life will change. In many ways you will no longer be the person you are. If you are still ready, we will begin the procedure," thought Researcher Zal.

****

Joel and Belinda followed Researcher Zal into a room bathed in a deep lilac light. It was like a scene from the movies as three aliens advanced toward them. Dr. Sta, they knew immediately that he was Dr. Sta, motioned for them to lie down on two separate operating tables and they watched as the three aliens took out long, searching, wafer-thin probes. Belinda looked up as the doctors alternated between Joel and herself. She could feel no pain, in fact she could feel no sensation at all.

"Joel," she thought. "I know who King Bayinnaung is."

They both lay inert as time passed. How long they had no idea. Their minds were opened to a new world as information flooded in. Hemingway, Tolstoy, Henri Bergson, Orwell and so many others, the arts, sport, geography, world leaders of the present and the past, so much detail and so much knowledge. They both slept for some considerable time as their dreams exploded in their heads. Belinda was riding a chariot, then flying through the air pursued by men with books. Joel sat and conversed with Abraham Lincoln under his statue at the Lincoln Memorial. Three earth days passed before they awoke.

"Joel," thought Belinda.

"I know so much!" thought a dumbfounded Joel. He pulled himself upright and smiled over at Belinda. "I understand now, I am a match for any man."

"I feel the same, my mind is racing," thought Belinda as Researchers Soa and Zal entered the room.

"Your human brains are capable of far more than you imagine. It has been a disappointment to us how little your use of the brain has improved over the eons. We have contrasted your development with ours and concluded that it was the battle for survival that did not permit you to develop as we did. On Niburu there is a plentiful supply of the delicious Alasay and an in-built respect for society and order. We were engaged in mental stimulation from birth while you, needing speech to communicate, found many other factors that you needed to consider," though Researcher Soa.

"I can see now that your I.Q is far in excess of ours," thought Belinda. "Even the great thinkers of our time must seem inadequate to you."

"I.Q is an earth measurement that lacks sophistication. Despite the limitations of your brains your great thinkers have detailed the theory of relativity, shown an understanding of advanced mathematics that we have learned from, and your literature has opened up a new world for us. In many ways we are in awe of you, not the other way around," thought Researcher Zal.

"On the other hand," interjected Captain Mir, using an earth synonym. "We look in barely disguised horror at the state of politics on your planet. Your adherence to the nation state is constraining the development of your species and allowing opportunists and those of low-intellect to rise high levels of office," thought Captain Mir.

"We place considerable value on democracy in our societies," thought Joel.

"A laudable concept but one flawed by self-interest and the ease in which voters can be manipulated, or even stopped from voting entirely. We, as thinkers, reach a consensus and action it. Our ruling council works solely on what is best for the planet and our species. That is our view for your planet," thought Captain Mir. "You already have regional or global organizations but their influence is kept limited as their potential success might harm the sovereignty of the nation state. They are starved of funds, or their warnings are dismissed by self-serving politicians with only a short-term outlook, that usually being their time in office."

"I understand what you are saying, but to change the views of politicians takes time, time we do not have," thought Belinda.

"Then we need to reach out beyond the politicians as Alessandra is doing. They are part of the problem as well as being part of the solution," thought Joel.

"What if the earth suffered a major famine, a pandemic or increasing flooding. Could that be better served with a global organization giving oversight, or by smaller nation states scrambling about on their own?" thought Researcher Zal.

"Your planet's environment issues will not be solved in the three short years you have left, but we need to see a willingness to change and we need to witness that change beginning. You have a huge task in front of you, one that we will monitor and support fully. Alessandra will be joining us on the spaceship shortly to undergo the same procedure that you yourselves have undergone. I envisage the others well be selected to join as their telepathic abilities become more pronounced," thought Captain Mir.

"You are looking to have more telepaths on the planet," thought Belinda.

"That is our consensus. The power of speech has enabled communication, but also deception in your species. This has been true since your race moved to settled society. We need to learn from the past also. Those with telepathic powers choose to rule and therein lies our dilemma, telepaths have an advantage over normal humans. The past has demonstrated to us that, even if they don't, they will be seen as abusers of power. We too must be careful about how we introduce telepathy into your society," thought Researcher Soa.

"We will remain to monitor your planet through the years to come. This spaceship does not have the capability to traverse space as far as Niburu," thought Researcher Zal.

"So, you gave up your lives to remain here," thought Belinda.

"That is true," thought Captain Mir. "By staying here, we have been rendered sterile. When the last of us dies then the earth will have a long wait until the next return of the Annunaki."

Chapter 7

One year passed.

"Alessandra, welcome to the International News Network. You have taken the world by storm with your environmental blog. We are one year in since you launched your 'Three-Years to Save the Planet,' campaign and I imagine you feel proud of what you have achieved?" said Susan Ryder.

"I followed a path that had been cleared for me by so many of our great, yet often unknown environmentalists, Julia 'Butterfly' Hill who sat in the branches of a redwood tree for almost two years in order to save it being cut down, the late Wangari Maathai from Kenya the founder of the Green Belt Movement, and Greta Thunberg to name just three. These names have been an inspiration for me as well as so many others, but I felt throughout my life that that environmental concerns were always on the outside looking in. I have looked to change that.

"In truth, I have achieved little. My team, and I single out Joel Atkins, Belinda Mineo, and Steffano Icardi have all worked miracles in getting our 'Three-Years to Save the Planet,' message out there. We have galvanized the young and the environmentally aware for which I am so grateful. We have teams in practically every country around the world cleaning up their environment and lobbying their governments to do more, but despite this groundswell of opinion the political classes seem to continue to view environmental issues from a distance to put it politely."

"Is that why you feel you have achieved little?" asked Susan.

"Don't get me wrong. The awareness this campaign has created staggers me. One year ago, I was a little-known blogger in Rome with a primarily European following. Now I have a following of over thirty million subscribers and growing, and with offices in twenty countries around the globe all working toward seeing environment issues addressed in their regions," replied Alessandra.

"That looks like an amazing success to me," said Susan.

"In terms of motivating people and raising awareness it is. People, everyday people going about their daily business, are increasingly supporting us. The environmental movement is not just the young and what the right-wing call 'tree-huggers', it has matured to become a more united, global force for change.

"In terms of growth and global awareness I feel the campaign has been unbelievably successful, in terms of changing the way governments perceive the importance of global environmental concerns, less so. The European Union stands head and shoulders above others in leading the way. The Green movement in Germany continues to grow and influence policy, but elsewhere politicians pay only lip-service to the environment," said Alessandra.

"Why do you think that is?" asked Susan.

"Money primarily and indifference to a degree. You only have to look at the money thrown by billionaires to undermine the climate change debate. It was about money and it was about profit. Our society is driven by greed, it should be driven by trying to form an equitable society and by finding a balance between us and the environment," said Alessandra.

"You didn't name anyone in particular?" said Susan.

"No, because I don't want to waste my time in meaningless litigation when there are so many serious issues to address," replied Alessandra. "Environmental issues are seen by many as an additional cost to business. More regulation, more form-filling, more people employed in areas that don't add value, the true reason is that caring for the planet costs money. It is also the right thing to do," said Alessandra. "We have one planet. It is an infinite resource. We are plundering below its surface, destroying its wildlife, desertifying its surface, and polluting its atmosphere. There has to come a tipping point and I don't see that as very far off."

"Alessandra you obviously feel very strongly about these issues. Do you think your movement can take the next step and make your dreams a political reality?" asked Susan.

"They are not dreams. To me and my followers they are what needs to be done to ensure the future survival of our planet. I prefer to keep out of political matters, my two directors, Joel Atkins and Belinda Mineo are far more expert and effective than I, however, the increasingly right-wing regimes that bedevil our planet at the moment seem to put profit before everything, before people and before the planet," replied Alessandra.

"'Three years to save the environment' is now one year in. How do you see the remaining two years going?" asked Susan.

"Our first objective was to continue to raise awareness, but more than that it was to engage with those outside the 'mainstream' environmental supporters and I feel we have been very successful in doing that. Our supporter base has an almost equal number of men and women from around the world. As I tell them, they are my ambassadors. They help me in taking the fight to their governments and, if necessary, forcing their government to act even if only through the ballot box.," said Alessandra.

"Alessandra, thank you so much for coming to talk with me today, and sharing your views on something that is clearly very important to you" said Susan.

"It was my pleasure, and thank you for inviting me. Before we go can I amend our slogan on your program?" asked Alessandra.

"Of course, you can," answered Susan.

"Two-Years to save the Planet," stated Alessandra.

****

Badr El-Din had spent nearly a year trying to get to America only to be thwarted by U.S. Immigration at every turn. He could sense Joel Atkins and Belinda Mineo and watched their rising profile with a fanaticism bordering on hatred but no matter how much he cursed they were out of his reach. He paid a smuggler to take him to Italy where Alessandra D'Angelo was waiting, but his container was intercepted and he was sent back to Damascus. When he arrived back, he could sense something had changed.

"Thinkers, thinkers, I can hear them, they are here in Damascus. They are weak though, but they are becoming aware," he thought. As he thought he looked back in time to when he met King Emenluana "The thinkers were here all along, the Middle East was their birthplace. It is here that they lurk, I will stop them."

"I am becoming increasingly concerned with Badr El-Din thought Researcher Soa. "He has tried and failed to reach our three leading telepaths but now he is sensing that others are awakening. He has vowed to himself to kill them."

"I think it may be linked to the history of the thinkers. Our research has shown that we were particularly strong in Mesopotamia and the early civilizations surrounding the Indus Valley but the people were instilled with violence against them and sought us out and killed those they could," thought Researcher Zal.

"It wasn't only the Indus Valley civilizations, the persecution of our kind appears to have been common in the east, particularly the region that became China," Researcher Soa.

"Why did the people turn on our kind. By the nature of telepaths, we are benign when compared with humans. We do not covet wealth or possessions, and are not prone to violence unless the provocation is severe," thought Captain Mir.

"We were different, that seems to be enough for humans. Look at the issues on their planet now. White versus black, Christians versus Muslims, rich versus poor, native born versus foreigner. There are so many threats that the humans perceive that can be built into confrontation. It is my contention that we were different and that was whipped up into jealousy and hated," thought Researcher Zal.

"You are saying that if the early humanoid we re-engineered to all be telepaths then the pogrom that took place against our people would not have occurred," thought Captain Mir.

"It is so many eons ago that it is difficult to know the minds of our early explorers. I imagine they felt that it would be enough to change the DNA in only some of the species with the anticipation that telepathic thought would pass through the species over time, not changing the species but enhancing them," thought Researcher Zal.

"It is clear that telepathic thought has passed down the generations although in small numbers. It is only our proximity that has awakened it," thought Researcher Soa. "More are awakening every day. At the moment we only allow our three original subjects to communicate with us on the spaceship, but we can now sense over one thousand telepaths with the ability to communicate over planet Earth."

"I know that Alessandra has placed some of them in her team offices and she praises them highly," thought Researcher Zal. "We have started the process of upgrading them. It is becoming clear to me that we need to establish many more telepaths on the planet in order to re-establish the integrity that is lacking in so many humans."

"I fear you are right, but I am concerned that the normal humans will treat the telepaths as different and we know how the humans can treat those they consider 'different,'" thought Captain Mir. "Nevertheless, I feel we must try. We will remain in this solar system for many years and can monitor the situation. I have arrived at the conclusion that, at the present time, the humans cannot manage their planet without our help. Unless something radical happens they, and their planet, are on a course for self-destruction."

"Then, they have two years to convince us otherwise," thought Researcher Soa.

"We will continue bring selected specimens to the spaceship in order to enhance their ability," thought Researcher Zal.

"And what of Badr El-Din?" thought Researcher Soa.

"We have learned all we can from him. He will kill unless he is exterminated. I will see to it," thought Captain Mir.

****

"To put it simply, there are too many humans on the planet," thought Researcher Pan. "We limit population growth on our planet through the mutuality of telepathic thought. We know and understand the limitations of Nibiru. We have studied and understand the optimum number of our species that can survive and live-in compatibility with our planet. The humans know of no such constraints."

"Their population is in excess of seven billion," thought Captain Mir.

"And rising relentlessly. Their own projections see over ten billion in total in the next thirty years," thought Researcher Pan.

"Surely, the planet cannot sustain that number," thought Captain Mir.

"They are, technologically speaking, a rapidly advancing species. The reason that their current population can survive is their ability to develop and harness technology to meet their needs and that has been the case throughout their history. They are an innovative species who face an obstacle and find a way to overcome it," thought Researcher Pan.

"And this 'innovation' you talk of, does it come at a cost to the planet," thought Captain Mir.

"In many cases, yes," thought Researcher Pan. "To sustain their growing population, they have plundered the resources of the planet at an ever-increasing rate, and in doing so have released excessive amounts of particulates that are damaging to the planet into its atmosphere thereby causing global temperatures to increase and damaging the optimum air quality for them as a species," thought Researcher Pan.

"Their solutions are short-term in nature," thought Captain Mir.

"Historically yes, but they are aware of the damage they are doing to their planet and are developing ways in which to mitigate their actions, but as we can see from our scans of the planet the results to date are minimal when judged on a global scale'" thought Researcher Pan.

"Why do they not do more," thought Captain Mir.

"Do more to stop the damage to their planet, or more to curb their population growth," thought Researcher Pan. "Both are destroying their planet, but I will look at the damage to their planet first."

"I am aware of your conversations with the other Researchers and have included my observations in detail in the report you can absorb while in stasis. Theirs is a rich planet in so many ways, it is conductive to life and has an abundance of minerals and resources that are easily harvested. It makes our planet of Niburu look poor by comparison. The humans they are unaware of what a unique planet they live on as to them it is the only habitable planet they know. It is only now that they are looking out into the cosmos and realizing what an inhospitable place it is to life.

"My report notes the political and cultural influences on their destruction of the planet as I feel these obstacles need to be overcome before any meaningful progress can be made on bringing the planet back from the precipice it is now on. Humans are greedy, and by that, I mean that they always seem to want more than another person. This is not true in all instances but is true in many. It is a concept we are unfamiliar with and has taken, not only myself, but other Researchers some time to grasp.

"One example that is particularly relevant to the destruction of the planet is the coal industry in the country they call the United States of America. In recent history the humans became aware of the damage they were doing to their planet by releasing the carbon caused by the burning of this fossil fuel into the atmosphere, in particular how the impact of their activities was having on the climate. Climate change, as they called it, was becoming accepted by people until some of those with a vested interest in coal commenced a campaign to debunk the science. Their interests were being threatened if society or industries moved away from coal. This is just one of many attacks that those seeking to address climate change have faced in recent years. Those who have money, and with it positions, power and the trappings that go with it in their society do not want to give them up."

"Even at the cost of their planet," thought Captain Mir.

"Even at the cost of their planet. Many humans place their own short-term needs above that of the planet. Damage to the planet is a problem for the future, not for now. Do not misunderstand me there are many humans fighting to make a difference but they are fighting vested interests with power that have often corrupted the political system for their own ends. Those who value the future well-being of their planet and their species are being constrained by those with the power and those they manipulate into following them," thought Researcher Pan.

"That is a situation that does not bode well for the future of the planet. We have already started to influence the thinking on the planet but I can see we need to do more," thought Captain Mir.

"Population growth is another issue that they are finding it difficult to face, although efforts have been made" thought Researcher Pan. "The People's Republic of China instituted as one child per family policy in an attempt to stem population growth but as boys are considered more valuable than girls it led to the death of many infant girls in order that that could have a boy in their family. For many parts of the globe, the regions which are kept in perpetual poverty in order to provide a cheap pool of labour for the rich, these people have more children as they are needed to farm the land and provide financial security for their parents in old age. The land often becomes denuded, wildlife is displaced or killed and a vicious cycle ensues. Not being able to make a living from the land the children make their way to the city where they often scrape a poor living and add to pollution and the degradation of the environment.

"The richer parts of the globe, which are generally in the northern hemisphere, are seeing a reduction in population as it is not economically viable for most of the poorer people in these countries to have more than two children. The numbers are being sustained by people from the poorer parts of the world, however, they are from a different culture and, often, religion, and may have poor communication skills. This is leading to cultural conflicts in these countries as those who are native to the country feel threatened, or are driven to feeling threatened for political gain," thought Researcher Pan.

"You are saying that their current population level is not sustainable," thought Captain Mir.

"It is sustainable but only at the cost of increasing use of the planet's resources and the complication that brings with it. They are a caring species and their medical advances have been quite spectacular, even by our standards, over the past century. The downside from a population perspective is that the people with access to these medical advances are living far longer than was the case only a short time ago," thought Researcher Pan.

"They have a short lifespan by our norms," thought Captain Mir.

"But as their young population continues to grow and the lives of the older population is extended the impact on population growth is profound. Their projected population growth may be sustainable but only at an ever-increasing cost to their planet," thought Researcher Pan.

"I look forward to absorbing your full report but I can see how unrestricted population growth is unacceptable to the well-being of the planet," thought Captain Mir. "It is an area that we will need to consider with care as we make our judgment on the future of this planet."

Chapter 8

"Maxie, whatever is the matter," asked DeVane.

"I keep hearing voices, voices in my head. I can't shut them out!" said Maximilian Browne.

"Honey, this has been going on too long. I will make an appointment with Dr. Schlesinger," said DeVane.

"But he's a psychiatrist. Do you think I'm going mad?" asked Maximilian.

"I don't know honey, but you can't keep going on like this. These noises in your head are getting louder every day. I'm worried for you," said DeVane.

The following day Maximilian tucked his beard to one side as he lay on the psychiatrist's leather couch.

"In your own words," said Dr. Schlesinger without preamble.

"I keep hearing voices, not any voices, I keep hearing the Annunaki," said Maximilian.

Dr. Schlesinger motioned for him to continue.

"You know me doctor. The Annunaki are my life. The history and the legends, they have been part of my life since childhood. Now I am hearing their voices but it is not the voices of the Annunaki I know."

"Tell me more about these voices?" asked Dr. Schlesinger.

"They are not really voices. It is as if someone is in my head thinking. Not just someone, many people. I don't know how to describe it," said Maximilian. "Sometimes there is one voices and sometimes hundreds. Even if there are hundreds, I can hear them all clearly."

"How do you know it is the Annunaki?" asked Dr Schlesinger.

"From what they are talking about," he replied.

"What are they talking about?" asked Dr. Schlesinger.

"Us, humans, they are researching us?" said Maximilian. "They think we are destroying the planet and they want us to stop, and there are earth people they talk to. It all gets so jumbled in my mind."

"What do the Annunaki sound like?" asked Dr. Schlesinger.

"They don't make a sound," replied Maximilian as he moved to sit on the edge of the psychiatrist's couch. He held his head in his hand and shook it vigorously from side-to-side. His long, black beard trailed to the floor. "They have no sound but I hear them. It is only from those on earth that I can hear a sound. I cannot make sense of it doctor."

"How long have you been hearing these voices?" asked the doctor.

"A little over a year," said Maximilian.

"When did you first hear them?" asked the doctor.

"I remember that clearly," said Maximilian. "I was giving my show in Chicago. I could hear two voices in the audience, one strong and one weak. Luckily, I have made the same presentation over a hundred times so was able to carry on, but I thought I was being questioned in some way. Since that day the voices have gradually became clearer and as they do, they frighten me," said Maximilian.

"Why?" asked the psychiatrist.

"Because they are here to destroy the Earth, they are here to destroy the Earth," he replied as he held his head in his hands and sobbed uncontrollably.

****

"Many of the humans are finally awakening to their telepathic powers," thought Researcher Soa. "There are over twenty thousand who have reached the initial stage of awakening and nearly a thousand who have the ability to communicate with us. Of the ones who have awakened to date, fifty-two per cent have been terminated as being unfit for our purpose."

"And Joel?" thought Captain Mir.

"Joel is unaware of the termination rate. He only hears from those that have been deemed acceptable. I know he became concerned when the telepath Badr El-Din ceased communication, but he put that thought to the back of his mind as he continued his work," thought Researcher Soa.

"Good, it is best that the humans are unaware that those telepaths with wrong thinking are being terminated," thought Captain Mir.

"Joel has organized a network of Environmental Action Centres, as he calls them, across the world. He has placed telepaths from the respective nations in charge and with the funds we have provided to him, he is making considerable impact in passing Alessandra's message around the world. She announced 'Two Years to Save the World' yesterday. I hope for their sake the humans take the message seriously." thought Researcher Soa.

"The humans have come a long way in the past year, both Joel and Alessandra seem to have struck a chord with those whose thinking is sound. The battle is to convince those whose views are obscured by self-interest or ignorance to think again and that will be no easy task," thought Captain Mir.

"The humans are far too easily swayed, but once they have decided they seem oblivious to any message that goes against their belief," thought Researcher Soa.

"It is their limited IQ's that restricts their ability for considered thought," thought Captain Mir.

"It is more than that, it is their nation, their upbringing and their education to name only three. I agree, the limited intelligence of humans in comparison to us is a problem," thought Researcher Soa.

"We have the ability to upgrade their IQ levels but the size of the task with seven billion on their planet is beyond the capabilities of this ship," thought Captain Mir.

"It is beyond the capabilities of the mother ship even if we recalled it," thought Researcher Soa.

"Then we must place our trust in Joel, Belinda and Alessandra and give them our full support over the next two years," thought Researcher Soa. "Joel is addressing a symposium on the environment in Alessandra's home city of Rome today. Alessandra and Belinda will be joining him. The entire event is being shown across all their global media channels. Joel intends to attack government complacency and Alessandra will highlight the 'Two Years to Save the Planet' message."

"The stimulation of his IQ level has shown the potential of humans. Joel's powers of understanding and synthesis of ideas demonstrates the ability of humans if we can advance then past this stage of their evolution," thought Captain Mir.

"We have upgraded over one thousand humans. As we can read their minds, we can understand them and their personalities better than they can. We can select only the best. It is shame that slightly over half have to be discarded as substandard," thought Researcher Soa.

"Their demise is painless and looks like a normal death, but the humans are an emotional species and the death of someone near to them, even if they are substandard, hurts them," thought Captain Mir.

"They are a caring species, but equally, a destructive species. To be allowed to continue to inhabit the planet they need to understand how to curb the destructive side of their nature," thought Researcher Soa.

"That will not be an easy task, destruction seems inherent in their nature," thought Captain Mir.

****

"Joel Atkins, Chief Operating Officer of Environmental Action, welcome the Lee Han show on the HK Broadcasting channel," said Lee Han. "Your co-partner in Environmental Action, Alessandra D'Angelo recently updated 'Three Years to Save the World' from three years to two. Why such as short-time frame?

"Because time is running out," said Joel. "Over the years we have set targets twenty or even fifty years into the future, and I accept that in certain industries that is the only practical approach, but fifty years is a long time and, as we have seen far too often dates are often pushed back as politics, in particular, intervenes. Our movement is about a different approach, one that has been tried before but we are fortunate in that we have the funding to challenge big business and the libertarian governments who deny climate change and the continued destruction of the global environment despite all the evidence to the contrary. Their denial of climate change has more to do with how they secure their funding and maintain their political stance and position."

"They would say that the entire climate change debate is nothing more than a hoax," remarked Lee Han.

"They would, wouldn't they?" said Joel. "Their interests are different from ours. They seek a world where capitalism is king and businesses prosper irrespective of the cost to people, wildlife or the environment. We seek a world that can live in peace with itself, a world in balance if you like."

"What do you mean by that?" asked Lee Han.

"To the businessman environmental action is a cost. Regulations that limit pollutants entering the atmosphere, restrictions of dumping waste in the ocean or in rivers, or movements away from profitable sectors such as coal to cleaner energy sources, just to give three obvious examples. The last forty years has shown how these 'businessmen' have corrupted public opinion by casting doubt of the scientific evidence and by linking environmental action with left-wing politics. Environmental action has no place in politics, it should be above one nation or a group of nations, politics. The evidence of climate change is indisputable, and those who have acted to discredit the argument for their own personal gain or through an almost blind devotion to a political doctrine, I personally hold in contempt."

"They are harsh words indeed," said Lee Han.

"Harsh words and words on the record. 'Two Years to Save the Planet', am I worried about offending the zealots that deny climate change or accept pollution as a price to pay, no way."

"You have recently returned from a field trip to Africa, what did you discover while you were there?" asked Lee Han.

"I have recently returned from Egypt where I journeyed down the Nile as part of a research project for Environmental Action. The trip was suggested by our office in Cairo as they regard the city and the country of Egypt as one of the main candidates in the way the needs of the planet are disregarded," commenced Joel. "I do not single out Egypt, as from what I have heard and observed first-hand, our disrespect for mother earth and the flora and fauna that graces it appals me.

"My concern is the environment and to me that has three aspects. The first is climate change which we are adding too every single day. I accept that the change of thinking needed to implement anything meaningful will take time and face many vested interests, but a change of thinking is needed.

"'Two Years to Save the Planet' has its primary focus on cleaning up the world. Our planet is in danger of becoming little better than a waste dump, there is a plastic island in the middle of the Atlantic, it's so big it is almost casually referred to as an island. My recent trip to Egypt was an eye opener in so many ways. The city of Cairo itself has trash strewn not only in the streets, but on top of buildings. The infrastructure to manage the waste has been simply overwhelmed to the point that the people of Cairo seem to have accepted this situation as the norm.

"Many of the tributaries that feed water into the Nile are clogged, and I mean clogged, mainly plastic waste. Fish ingest the plastic as it breaks down and, in consequence, it enters the human food chain. I am not talking about the odd bottle of plastic waste; I am talking about the tributaries often at a standstill because the waste is so great. This is the case along huge lengths of the Nile," said Joel.

"You also visited Kenya?" asked Lee Han.

"For a different reason, and my third aspect to environmental action. I went there to see the wanton destruction of endangered wildlife either for food, or for medicines for the rich economies, particularly in the east. To see the carcass of a recently killed Rhino with only its tusk removed as the flies started to gather must rank of one of the saddest sights of my visit. Fortunately, this Rhino did not leave an infant to perish as is often the case as I was informed."

"Two Years to Save the Planet. What do you hope to achieve?" asked Lee Han.

"In the remaining two years we hope to achieve great advances. If the first year, and the response to Alessandra's blog is anything to go by, we have galvanized across the generations. We have offices establish across the globe that act, not only on our global objectives, but on local initiatives. Our managers have been chosen for their honesty and integrity and take it from me they are not afraid to challenge authority when they must. We will not save the planet just by being nice, we will save it by the committed support of people all the way up from the grass-roots level. We work with other organizations in order to maximize our combined resources and knowledge. We are a new operation and we still have much to learn.

"What do I hope to achieve? A change of mindset. That it is not acceptable to continue as we are and that it is not acceptable for short-term political and profit objectives to override the needs of the planet. As we venture into space, we see how hostile the cosmos is. We are constantly discovering new planets, none of them hospitable to life as we know it. We have a gem of a planet and we are the custodians of it, and from where I am sitting, we are doing a damn poor job of it," Joel concluded.

****

Marcia rolled over and watched her man. Clyde lay on the bed staring at the ceiling fan as it made a slight mechanical whirr that broke the silence of the bedroom.

"I've got to tell you something," he said. "I have kept it a secret for over a year."

She nudged him as if to say go on.

"Understand, this is big. This will lead to the biggest story of your career and, probably, the end of mine," he said as he leaned over and faced her. "I think there are aliens on Mars, and I am convinced they are the Annunaki."

"You're kidding!" she replied.

"No, I'm not, I'm deadly serious," he said as he told her the entire story beginning with the loss of the New Horizons probe.

"Is it okay if we go downstairs for a coffee and I can record all this?" she asked.

"No problem. I need you to get this right. To keep this from you for the past year has been hard enough but now I have made my decision to tell you I want it to be right in every detail," said Clyde.

"How will Bill and Jenny react?" Marcia asked.

"Not well I fear, although I know they are both struggling with whether they should tell anyone," Clyde replied.

"They both know?" Marcia asked.

"We worked it out together although I came up with the method that could prove that there could be a spaceship on Mars. The fact they were the Annunaki is nothing but speculation on my part, but with the increase in activity about them as we near 2022, the year of their supposed return I don't think it is too far of a stretch, particularly now the existence of aliens has finally been admitted," he said. "I will tell you the full story now and then go and tell them. I don't know how they will react as they have kept the secret for well over a year. Name me as the source and don't mention anyone else," said Clyde.

That morning, like all weekday and some weekend mornings, Clyde walked in to the New Horizon's Operations Room at NASA.

"Boss, Jenny can I have a word?" he asked. Curious at the formality of the request they both gathered around. "I've told Marcia about the Annunaki."

"Thank God," said Bill Manners. "Shall I tell, shan't I tell it's been tearing me up for the past year." Jenny simply kissed him on the cheek and said "Good."

"You know we will probably all lose our jobs for this?" said Clyde.

"Probably," replied Bill. "I'm off to see Johnathon Langerhans, our Administrator. Are you coming with me?"

"All for one," said Jenny

"Marcia said that she wouldn't release her piece in the Orlando Guardian until I have read it and agreed it. We have some time but not much," said Clyde.

"Well, he didn't really know what to say," said Clyde, one of the three newly suspended NASA scientists. Let's put New Horizons in neutral until whoever takes over from us moves in."

"And I'll buy you both a coffee after they escort us from the premises" said Bill.

Aliens on Mars!

... ran the banner headline together with all the details that Joel has passed to his long-time lover. Suddenly everything was wiped off of every front page. No more presidential tweets, no more Brexit, and no more reality show celebrities, the Annunaki dominated everything. Are they really there? Does the science prove anything? What are they doing? Why are they waiting until 2022? Are they coming to kill us? Is God with them? Do they look like on the movies? Underground shelters available now!

Chapter 9

"I am outside the Atlanta home of Maximilian Browne who was found dead in an apparent suicide last night. His long-term partner DeVane Wilson called police shortly after 11.30 last night when she returned home after visiting a friend in Miami," said Mickie Carmichael of the Atlanta News Network. "I see that behind me the detective in charge of the investigation is leaving the house with De Vane."

"Good Morning, ladies and gentlemen. My name is Detective William Ortega of the Atlanta police department. The body of Maximilian Browne was found last night by his wife after she returned from a night visiting a friend. He died by a gunshot wound to the head in an apparent suicide, foul play is not suspected. Mr. Browne's long-time partner De Vane would like to take this opportunity to say a few words and we would be grateful if you leave her to grieve in peace after she has answered your questions."

"Thank you, Detective Ortega. Maxie was a wonderful man and a man larger than life. He is known to you all as the narrator of the Annunaki story, to me he was much more. In recent months we both became concerned about his mental health. Maxie told me of hearing voices in his head, he said they were the voices of the Annunaki, but not the Annunaki he knew through legend. He sought professional advice but still kept hearing the voices. I fear they drove him to take his own life. Thank you, I will not be taking questions," said De Vane.

"De Vane, do you know what he made of yesterday's news that the Annunaki are thought to have established a base on Mars," said Mickie Carmichael.

"The police think he killed himself in the early morning, long before the news broke," De Vane said as she turned and went back inside the house.

****

Johnathan Langerhans, William Manners, Jenny Claybourne, and Clyde Whittaker sat facing the press with the NASA logo behind them. The world was watching.

"Good afternoon, Ladies, Gentlemen and members of the press. In the light of revelations recently announced in the press we have convened this press conference in order to clarify and answer any questions you have regarding to yesterday's press stories of a spaceship being found on Mars. I have asked my team to be completely honest and transparent and answer all your questions fully and as comprehensively as possible.

"Like yourselves I only found about this yesterday when the team to my left came to my office and revealed their findings and their thinking on the matter. By then, this story had been given to the press. I hand you over to Joel Atkins who broke the story," said Johnathan.

"Thank you, Mr. Administrator, and I would like to say at the outset that I apologize to yourself and NASA for breaking the story as I did, and also to my co-workers Bill and Jenny who I placed in an impossible situation. Over a year ago I discovered a magnetic anomaly on the Martian surface. I speculated that this could be the tell-tale sign of a spaceship and decided to research further. My thinking was that this was an Annunaki spacecraft and my logic behind that, if you can call it logic, was to do with the disappearance and reappearance of the New Horizons probe. No plausible scientific reason could be given for why the New Horizons probe vanished for three months only to suddenly reappear traveling on the same course and same speed as it was when it disappeared. As Sir Arthur Conan Doyle famously said 'Once you eliminate the impossible, whatever remains, no matter how improbable, must be the truth'. The only solution was that the spaceship had been interfered with by an outside force and, to my mind, that force had to be extra-terrestrial," opened Joel.

"I speculated that the New Horizons probe had been intercepted shortly after it had completed its primary mission, that of investigating and photographing the Pluto-Charon system. I then asked myself why and the only plausible answer was that the extra-terrestrials were examining the probe to see how advanced our civilization was. They also had the capability to release the probe on its same course and trajectory. Why would they release it? Because they were moving from their location. Where would they go? There choices are limited. They could set down on some of the moons of Jupiter or Saturn but, if they were to visit Earth then Mars seemed a more likely stopping off point.

"From there my mind wondered. I was convinced by this time that if they were extra-terrestrials then they must be the Annunaki. There prophesied return in 2022 and the increase in activity surrounding them made it clear to me that we were dealing with them. I researched the data on the Internet only to find that activity surrounding the Annunaki peaked as a certain event occurred. That event was when a certain longitude of Mars was closest to Earth. I searched along that line of longitude on the Martian surface and discovered the magnetic anomaly that I saw as evidence of the presence of the Annunaki on Mars. Over the past year I have scoured all photographic evidence from our satellites above the Martian surface but found nothing at the site of the magnetic anomaly, which is what I would expect."

"You haven't actually seen the spacecraft?" interrupted Peter Duckworth of the L.A. Chronicle.

"No, and I would expect to," replied Joel. "Any civilization as advanced as the Annunaki would have the ability to shield their spaceship from our prying eyes."

"Why now?" asked Peter.

"Both Bill Manners and Jenny agreed with my findings and supported the speculation that led to it. In truth it all sounded so outlandish that we decided to keep quiet. Over the past year we went about our lives as if nothing had happened, but it had. I became more and more convinced that what I had speculated was in fact true, and I think Bill and Jenny had arrived at the same conclusion. My partner works for the Orlando Guardian and yesterday I told her the story. It was too important not to tell. I did not tell Bill and Jenny what I had done until after I had done it. I understood that I might be laughed out of court, but she supported me and released the story. Marcia is at the back of the auditorium, usually in the front row. Like me she is concerned about the response.

"If your speculation is true, why do you think the Annunaki are here?" asked Peter Duckworth.

"Following President Obama's revelation that aliens have visited our planet many times in the past and that the Annunaki, in particular, are known to us through history, as is the date of their return, I would speculate that they are checking up on us. They captured New Horizons to examine it as they wanted to see how far we have advanced technologically. It wouldn't surprise me if they were watching this telecast now. I don't think they are here to launch an invasion as some of the more lurid papers and television channels are saying. I think they are here to check out our progress," answered Clyde.

"To what end?" asked Peter Duckworth.

"That I can only speculate on," said Clyde.

"And if you are wrong?" asked Peter.

"Then history will judge me poorly," replied Clyde.

****

"They know we are here," thought Researcher Soa. "A very clever deduction on his part. To use their phrase, it is not often we are outsmarted."

"I would like to meet this Clyde Whittaker," thought Captain Mir. "He is not a telepath but he is an intellectually advanced specimen. We will visit the planet next year and it would not hurt if the humans are aware of that fact in advance. If we have an ambassador with standing then that will prove useful."

"His standing is low at the moment," thought Researcher Soa.

"But it will rise dramatically when he is proven correct," thought Captain Mir.

****

Clyde opened his eyes to a quietness he had never heard before. He was conscious of the sound of is heartbeat. The air was fresh, like a spring morning with just a hint of rain in the air. He was in a bare room tinted a silvery lilac blue, but he was relaxed. He instinctively knew where he was.

"Good morning Clyde, welcome to Mars," thought Researcher Soa. "I am Researcher Soa and I am Annunaki."

He sat up on the corner of the bed. The gravity was lighter than Earth, but greater than that of Mars.

"You have artificial gravity," he said.

"It is attuned to our home planet of Nibiru which is slightly less than your Earth. I hope you do not find it too uncomfortable," thought Researcher Soa.

"I find it stimulating," he said. Suddenly the silvery blue tint lessened and Clyde was able to take in a panoramic view of the Martian landscape. He walked over to the window and touched it expecting to feel glass, although it was clear it felt like titanium.

"Mars, this is like a dream come true for me. Ever since I was a child I ventured into space, and now that dream has come true," he said. Researcher Soa stood alongside him as he gazed out for at least five minutes.

"You don't seem surprised to be here," she thought.

"You need to make contact and I am an obvious choice," said Clyde.

"Indeed, you are," thought Captain Mir as he entered the room. "You have fame, even notoriety and you are highly intelligent. We value intelligence in our culture.

"We value being seven feet tall and throwing balls in baskets," said Clyde.

"Therein lies a basic difference between us," thought Captain Mir as he indicated for Clyde to walk alongside him. The doors opened a la Star Trek and Clyde found himself in a room with one other Annunaki and four humans. He knew Researcher Zal immediately as he did Joel Atkins, Belinda Mineo, Steffano Icardi and Alessandra D'Angelo.

"How do I know you all?" he asked.

"We are telepaths and the strength of our combined thoughts have stimulated and awoken the DNA we planted in your ancestors over fourteen million of your Earth years ago. There is little of the original DNA remaining within you but while you are amongst us you will be a telepath. When you return to Earth you will be as before," thought Researcher Zal.

"Steffano, you were like me," said Clyde still awestruck by his ability to communicate telepathically and only slowly coming to terms with the fact that he knew these people intimately despite only just having met them.

"I have been enhanced by the Annunaki so that my brain is more efficient and I also have the ability to communicate telepathically," thought Steffano.

"You didn't move your lips," said Clyde.

"There is no need," thought Steffano. "You will adjust quickly."

"We thought that in honour of you all visiting us we would use a table and chairs as is the convention on Earth," thought Captain Mir.

Joel tapped the table. "What is it made of?" he asked.

"Molecules," thought Captain Mir.

"Joel, as you know we three are Annunaki, of the four humans here three carried enough of the telepathic gene that we implanted in your ancestors to regain their abilities earlier than others. Steffano has had his dormant genes reawakened and is now fully capable of telepathic communication," thought Researcher Soa.

"I have had my I.Q increased to the Annunaki standard of 250 by earth measurements. I am not unique in this, as of today nearly eighty thousand people have been selected to undergo the same process that I did," thought Steffano. "You can hear their thoughts for yourself."

Clyde marvelled. He could.

"Next year we will return to the Earth. We have a decision to make and I hope you will aid us in making that decision. The dilemma we are facing is do we recognize that our role in altering the DNA of early humanoids was in error and the resultant human species has proven itself unworthy of remaining the dominant species on the planet, or do we work alongside the humans in order to stop what we see as the inevitable destruction of their planet," thought Captain Mir.

"And do they genuinely have the will to change if we do help them," thought Researcher Soa.

"It is not an easy decision. We have spent the past three years in your solar system gathering all the relevant history of your planet and its peoples, in order to make the correct choice. It is a test we apply to all the many civilizations that we have nurtured, but be aware that in many cases we have made the decision to admit our failures and begin again. Our protocols are strict on this. Either we find that with our assistance your planet has the potential to thrive and prosper with the human species on it, or not," thought Researcher Soa.

"And what would be the fate of the human species if you decided that we do not meet your criteria?" asked Clyde.

"The human species would be expunged, only your infrastructure would remain. It only requires the combined thought of the crew to achieve this, nothing more," thought Researcher Soa.

"I understand why Belinda, Steffano and Joel are here, but why am I here?" asked Clyde.

"While you are on our spaceship you will listen to, and absorb the thoughts that surround you. You understand us already as your mind is not closed," thought Researcher Zal.

"You are here to save the planet. That is your motivation. Your decision whether to save the human race is secondary," said Clyde.

"Your planet is a jewel in our galaxy. We have encountered no other planet that can rival it. You have a temperate climate, ample resources and sufficient water, and it lies within a largely stable solar system. We have journeyed across the galaxy for over twenty million years and your planet is, by far the most beautiful and life-sustaining we have ever encountered," thought Captain Mir.

"And we are destroying it," thought Clyde.

"You are destroying the planet, the atmosphere, the wildlife and the flowers and plants that make your planet Earth a paradise, and you are doing this in the knowledge that you are doing it," thought Captain Mir.

"Joel, Alessandra, Steffano, and Belinda are here today to meet you. They know each other well as they are telepaths and are in constant communication," thought Researcher Zal.

"Being a telepath requires that you filter out extraneous thoughts but we all found that was a skill we gained earlier following the awakening of our ability," thought Joel.

"We need you to help us," thought Captain Mir. "There are now many telepaths on Earth. All have been selected for their character. Please appreciate we know those we upgrade to telepaths very well before we make any decision regarding their individual futures, it is one ability that telepaths hold dear.

"I have watched you and I understand you. I know of your love for your planet and your curiosity about what lies beyond. We need an ambassador for the day we arrive on earth. We will not enhance your telepathic ability as that would make your thinking favour us. We need you to be an arbiter between us and your race," thought Captain Mir.

"But I am no politician," thought Clyde.

"And from what we have seen from your politicians that is in your favour. We require of an arbiter someone who can be evenly balanced and not easily swayed but can talk and explain to the people. You are our choice if you accept the task," thought Captain Mir.

"Then I accept the task," said Clyde.

"Good," thought all those around the table.

"Joel, Belinda, Steffano, and Alessandra will return with you to push the message 'One Year to Save the Planet." We would normally blank anything that happens on the spaceship from your mind, but your memories and understanding of us will be left intact. Belinda has agreed to act as your liaison until we arrive. One year to save the planet," thought Captain Mir.

As they all rose from the table it, and the chairs surrounding it, simply disappeared.

"Molecules, they are reverting to their natural state as our minds can no longer hold them together. Would you like to walk on Mars before you return?" thought Captain Mir.

Chapter 10

January 1st, 2022.

A freezing New York woke up to the sight of a vast, blue-tinted silvered spaceship sitting silently in the sky above the United Nations Building and Manhattan.

"The Annunaki are punctual, I'll give them that," drawled a New Yorker as he looked up.

"Why are they here?" said another New Yorker.

"Do you mean here? They want to talk, but they want to talk to the United Nations and not some jumped up politician is my guess," drawled the New Yorker. "Oh, you mean why are they here on Earth? Who knows, but it doesn't look good."

****

Clyde Whittaker was on a split-screen with Elsa McDonald on the morning show.

"Clyde it seems as though you were right all along. The Annunaki spaceship has appeared this morning above the United Nations building in New York. Why do you think they are here?" asked Elsa.

"I know why they are here," said Clyde. "They have already been in contact with me."

"Been in contact, but how?" asked an open-mouthed Elsa.

"They want me to be their link with our species, as I understood them and worked out where they were. They are a species that understand and appreciate intelligence. They have been studying our civilization for over the three years that they have been in our Solar System," said Clyde.

"Are they here to destroy us?" asked a rather jittery Elsa.

"They could have done that already. No, they are concerned about us, but more than that they are concerned about the planet and the damage we are doing to it," replied Clyde.

"You talk as thought you have spoken with them?" asked Elsa.

"In a manner of speaking I have," said Clyde. "I know this all sounds bizarre, but so did my contention that the Annunaki were on Mars. I was vilified for that conclusion, and I daresay it will be the same for my claim that I have communicated with them. They intend to address a full session of the United Nations; they have no intention of communicating with politicians as their study of the planet has made them hold the majority of politicians in disdain. They will address the United Nations and they will address everyone on earth at the same time."

****

The world leaders had gathered. They didn't understand why they were here at this time and place, but they knew they had to be there. Suddenly, four aliens in a line were in their midst. They appeared to glide, their silvered-lilac gowns seemingly an inch from the ground. At first a novelty, like watching Star Trek, but soon the reality began to creep in. The Aliens looked benign enough, but there was a menace in their presence. The great and good of world politics began to pick up on the seriousness of their situation, and like the rest of the world were awed into silence. The Annunaki commenced to speak but their lips did not move.

"We, the Annunaki, are an ancient species who explore the galaxy much as your early voyagers discovered your planet. Our planet Niburu is dry and desolate when compared to your Earth but it supports and nurtures us, as your planet does you.

The Annals of the Annunaki record our first visit to your planet over forty million of your years ago. The Ducaz, the explorers, recorded a verdant planet bursting with life both on land and in the oceans. The records indicate that the planet was considered exceptional amongst the many planets they had visited and that it offered considerable potential for an advanced civilization to develop.

As our technology developed, we were able to visit your planet, and many others, on a cycle that is the equivalent of one million of your years. Over fourteen million years ago we considered options from the life on your planet to enhance in brain development and communications. We chose your ancestors and altered your DNA in order that, humans, as you have become, would be both the most intelligent and dominant beings on your planet.

We are recorded in your history as myth and legend and we are represented in your films and books. Our presence has left an imprint on your society. That was never our intention.

We have been studying your planet in detail for the past three years. First, as the astronomer Clyde Whittaker proposed from the Pluto-Charon system and, more recently, from Mars. We have been studying all aspects of your civilization, it's history, it's politics, it's culture, and its technological advancement, among many others. As a complex society you have much to be credited with, however there is much that concerns us.

Our society places strictures on our exploration and the results that come from it. The Earth is but one of over sixty civilizations that we have helped to advance. Of those fifty-one have prospered, and nine have been terminated. It is not life that is important to us. Life is commonplace within our galaxy and, we assume throughout the Universe. What is important is finding inhabitable planets and encouraging the development of advanced lifeforms who can thrive and co-exist with their planets. Our primary interest is that your planet remains viable for life into the future.

You have been blessed with the most wonderful planet we have ever seen in our millennia of travels throughout the galaxy, and you are destroying it at an increasingly alarming rate. You pollute the atmosphere, you destroy the flora and fauna that helps maintain your planet, you dispose of your waste matter without regard to its environmental impact, and you have a disparity in wealth across your world that brings shame on you.

Our concern is not your well-being or the survival of your species, it is first and foremost the well-being of your planet. If you are unable or unwilling to radically improve your interaction with the planet and convince us that the changes you make are sustainable then you will be terminated from the planet and we will choose another species that will, over time, come to dominate. That is the role laid down to us by our Ruling Council many millennia ago.

We are not here to destroy, but our mission has become one of saving you from yourselves. You already have the understanding to save your planet, but you ignore it in the relentless greed that affects so many in your society. Today is January 1, 2022, we will make our judgment on the future of your species on December 31, 2022. We have watched the activities of your environmentalists and they are correct in what they say. Learn from them and take the appropriate action. You have one year to make a meaningful change, or your species will be terminated from this planet.

We will communicate with Clyde Whittaker as your ambassador. We have no wish to communicate directly with your political leaders," thought Captain Mir.

The message went out, not only to the world leaders gathered in the United Nations Building, but to every person around the world and in their native tongue.

****

The Annunaki stood to one side as Clyde Whittaker, Joel Atkins, Belinda Mineo, Steffano Icardi and Alessandra D'Angelo moved to the podium.

There was discord among the ranks of the world leaders. Some moved to leave with barely concealed curses and a call to 'nuke 'em' and who do they think they are? The majority remained.

"Let them go," thought Captain Mir. "This is for your world to solve and solve quickly."

As order was regained Clyde got up to speak.

"The Annunaki have asked me to be their ambassador. I have been to their spaceship and have gained an understanding of both them and their motivation. Their objective is to see humans and the planet existing compatibly. If we cannot find a way then they will do as they say. They will terminate every human on the face of the planet and sow the seeds for a new species to grow in intelligence and assume our role.

I introduce Joel Atkins, Belinda Mineo, and Alessandra D'Angelo of Environmental Action, a grouping of the world's leading environmental organizations. They have been working with the Annunaki for the past three years to ensure the preparation of a plan of action for you to consider. I say consider, but what I really mean is adopt.

Let's be clear on this. I am not a politician; I am merely the person selected by the Annunaki to press home their demands. I use the term demands purposefully, because that is what they are, demands. Unless you as world leaders meet those demands, or make enough progress toward them to convince the Annunaki of a meaningful change the human race will be no more.

You need to put away your petty nationalism and think globally. Why are we at the United Nations today? Because the only way to achieve global unity on their demands is to act globally and strengthen world bodies such as this rather than starve them of funds and use them as a political whipping boy to suit the needs of individual politicians.

I hand you over to Joel Atkins, the CEO of Environmental Action.

"Our slogan is now 'One Year to Save the Planet" and it has never been truer. We have been working to put in place a practical plan that builds on our organization's objectives over the past two years and the achievements of the many environmentalists that work alongside us, and who have preceded us. Our plan is being made available as we speak. It is also being made available globally. We will now take questions against the backdrop of 'One Year to Save the Planet'."

The Annunaki were no longer beside them. The human race was on its own.

****

President Eustace Patricio was the newly elected president of Angola, and a telepath. Angola, like many other countries, had acted quickly to put in place governments sympathetic to the environmental issues raised and to work towards achieving them. Some countries have moved quickly, while others had not moved at all.

One month later the United Nations assembled again. There was no consensus. Populist presidents continued unabashed after what they had seen and heard while other nations moved only gradually toward change.

"What is there to understand?" asked President Eustace Patricio as he made his maiden speech. "We have until the end of the year to make meaningful changes that are sufficient to make the Annunaki realize that we are serious in our short-term and long-term obligation to clean up the planet. I have sat here today listening with increasing frustration as presidents and prime ministers go on about the effect on their economy and unemployment. Behind the facade of the podium speeches, I have listened as so-called world leaders talk about how to destroy the Annunaki. You cannot destroy them. They are millions of years ahead of us in technology.

If we do not come together on a global level and very quickly, we face the annihilation of our species. That is the reality of the situation. The politics of yesterday is exactly that. We need to move forward to face this threat to our existence and to improve our interaction with the planet. We must address the root causes of environmental degradation for the sake of all who live on it. Not just the rich countries of the world with their hedonistic lifestyles but with the entire population of the world. If the leading countries of the world cannot face up to the serious changes, they face in order to meet the challenges laid down by the Annunaki, then we will all be meeting our God sooner than we thought."

****

"There are three months to go and the Annunaki are blocking us out of their thought process," thought Joel.

"They said they would not make any decision until the end of the year," thought Alessandra.

"Then it would seem we are not to be permitted input into their decision-making process," thought Joel.

"The world is facing a crossroads," thought Alessandra. "There are riots across the globe and many people are growing increasingly frustrated by the stance their governments are taking."

"What will the Annunaki make of that," thought Belinda. "That people care, or that people are genuinely frightened."

"Both I fear. The Annunaki have studied us in detail for the past three years. They know our strengths and our weaknesses, and they know that while some of us will fight for the planet with our dying breath, and that others care only for themselves. By halting communication with us they are making it clear that it their decision and not ours. All we can do is wait," thought Alessandra.

"Wait and continue to put pressure for change on everyone who will listen. Remember we don't have solve all the planet's environmental issues but we need to show them a change in thinking, and a will to do what is right and clean up our planet and its atmosphere," thought Belinda

"Maybe it will go the wire. The Annunaki are aware we have the capability to save our planet. What they want to see is do we have the will to do so," thought Joel.

****

"Close all the lower decks!" thought the Commodore.

"The Indians are attacking the stasis chamber," thought Navigator Lon. "We must send in the cavalry to force them back. If they destroy the stasis chamber then we will never be able to get back to Niburu."

The commodore knew it was a lost cause.

A cowboy sauntered into view. "Where y'all goin' Sheriff," he thought.

"To the saloon, the Indians are attacking the stasis chamber, "thought the Commodore.

"I'd better mosey on down there," thought the cowboy.

The commodore entered the secure 'Thought Room'.

"Captain Mir, the mothership is lost," thought the Commodore. "The human thinking has spread like a pestilence among the crew. The crew have formed into two gangs, the Crips and the Bloods, and are fighting each other on the lower decks and on the upper decks cowboys are fighting Indians."

"You will have to destroy the mothership and us along with it. We cannot allow the human pestilence to get into the thought range of Niburu," thought Captain Mir.

"The termination has been authorized," said the Commodore.

There was loud noise and then silence.

The telepaths all awoke with a start, it was as if a gun had exploded in their heads.

"They've gone!" thought Joel. The only voices he could hear were from his fellow telepaths on earth.

"The spaceship it's still there, but there's no one on board," thought Alessandra.

"The mothership destroyed itself. We had infected them and they could not stop the spread of our culture throughout their vessel. They could not allow the spaceship to continue and risk spreading the infection," thought Joel.

"I cannot read any thoughts from the spaceship over the United Nations Building," thought Belinda. "It appears that all inside were killed when they destroyed along with the mothership."

****

"What do you mean communication from the Annunaki ship has stopped?" asked the President.

"Simply that. There has been no contact for the past two days," said his Secretary of Defence.

"And the spaceship is still there?" the president asked.

"Still positioned over the U.N. Building as it has been all along," replied the Secretary of Defence.

"Get choppers up there and take a look inside. With a bit of luck, they are all dead," said the President. "And put the CIA and FBI on alert to pick up those environmentalists who addressed the United Nations. If they have gone then we can put an end to all this nonsense and get back to business as normal."

****

"What do we do now," thought Alessandra.

"If the Annunaki are gone then they will come looking for us. The major powers, the ones that have fought the most vigorously against our environmental agenda will want to see us gone. They won't care if we become martyrs, they will simply want to lop the head off of the beast," thought Joel.

Their minds were swamped with offers of sanctuary from around the globe. The Annunaki may have gone but over one hundred thousand telepaths remained to spearhead the fight for the planet.

"We get our passports, say goodbye to our friends, and go. I will contact Clyde as he is not a telepath and he is not privy to what has happened to the Annunaki," thought Joel.

"We can communicate readily. The fight to save the planet goes on, with or without the Annunaki," thought Alessandra.

Printed in Great Britain
by Amazon